"Now I Know Why You've Been Single So Long Jeremy,"

Maddy declared sagely. "Taking you on would require a very strong-minded woman, and you've never found one who's been willing or able to go the full fifteen rounds with you."

"I'm not single," he reminded her tersely. "I'm married to a woman who doesn't even have enough guts to enter the ring."

Maddy gasped at this unexpected attack. "That was a low blow, Jeremy Kincaid!"

"Well, it's the truth, isn't it? You want me just as much as I want you, but you don't have the courage to do anything about it, *Mrs.* Kincaid."

"That's not true!"

"Then come here and show me," he suggested in a tone so seductive that Maddy felt the blood heating in her veins, and felt her desire for him igniting so quickly that it stunned her.

The sudden change in his behavior knocked her completely off balance. "I don't think—"

"Then don't think."

Dear Reader:

It's summertime, and I hope you've had a chance to relax and enjoy the season. Here to help you is a new man—Mr. August. Meet Joyce Thies's *Mountain Man*. He thinks he's conquered it all by facing Alaska, America's last frontier... but he hasn't met his mail-order bride yet!

Next month will bring a special man from Dixie Browning. Mr. September—Clement Cornelius Barto—is an unusual hero at best, but make no mistake, it's not just *Beginner's Luck* that makes him such a winner.

I hope you've been enjoying our "Year of the Man." From January to December, 1989 is a twelve-month extravaganza at Silhouette Desire. We're spotlighting one book each month with special cover treatment as a tribute to the Silhouette Desire hero—our *Man of the Month*!

Created by your favorite authors, these men are utterly irresistible. Don't let them get away!

Yours,

Isabel Swift
Senior Editor & Editorial Coordinator

JOYCE THIES
Mountain Man

Silhouette Desire

Published by Silhouette Books New York

America's Publisher of Contemporary Romance

SILHOUETTE BOOKS
300 East 42nd St., New York, N.Y. 10017

Copyright © 1989 by Joyce Thies

ISBN: 0-373-05511-0

First Silhouette Books printing August 1989

Printed in the U.S.A.

JOYCE THIES

considers the frontier days the most notable and romantic period in American history, and has always admired those courageous pioneers who left civilization behind in order to explore and homestead the vast wilderness territories. Her fascination with that colorful era prompted her to write several historical romances, but until she began researching sites for her twenty-third contemporary novel, she'd assumed that those thrilling days of yesteryear were long over. However, as soon as she came upon the words, "A land that has never known a human footprint," she realized that an American frontier still exists in the state of Alaska.

Her next task was to create the kind of man who would trade his luxurious condominium for a rustic log cabin, his briefcase for a shotgun and his expensive wing tips for snowshoes. "Jeremy Kincaid is that man," Joyce says. "He's a modern-day Davy Crockett who has the courage to laugh at himself and who possesses the strength of character necessary to share his life with an equally strong-minded woman. Jeremy could hold his own with any of my intrepid historical heroes, which to my way of thinking, makes him twice as romantic."

To my daughter, Melissa,
for continually reminding me
what love is all about

One

Big Sal's Roadhouse boasted the best mooseburgers in Alaska, but Jeremy Kincaid wasn't hungry. As he downed a cup of tea that was strong enough to blacken tin, he wondered for the tenth time in as many minutes just how he'd gotten himself into this terrible fix. He wasn't the impetuous type. The only risks he ever took were financial, affecting the size of his bank account—not the way he lived his life. Yet, according to the license in his hand, today was his wedding day. *His wedding day!*

With a sick feeling in the pit of his stomach, Jeremy glanced around at his surroundings, then back at the piece of paper in his hand. It was the only visible proof he had that his marriage was definitely scheduled to take place. Big Sal's might provide a decent bunk and the cheapest food a man could buy anywhere along the Dalton Highway, but the popular truck stop didn't bear the slightest resemblance to a wedding chapel, and the majority of the waiting guests were already half tanked on tap beer.

Moreover, Jeremy doubted that his prospective bride was going to appreciate having a thrice-married, six-foot-tall, snaggletoothed maid of honor, who in all likelihood would chain-smoke unfiltered Camels throughout the ceremony. Unfortunately, Big Sal was the only semirespectable female within a hundred-mile radius, and she was probably right in saying that a sweet, wholesome farm girl like Madelaine would want another woman present when she spoke her vows.

Vows! Jeremy closed his eyes and stifled a groan. Before now, he hadn't thought much about that part of marriage. A wedding involved making a solemn pledge in public, repeating promises before God!

No way was he prepared to do that! No matter how good Madelaine Price sounded on paper or looked in the snapshot she'd sent him, he couldn't promise to have and to hold a woman he'd never met, to love her from this day forward, for richer or poorer, in sickness and in health, until the day he died. No way!

With that conclusion firmly resolved in his mind, Jeremy poured himself another cup of strong, black tea and chugged it down fast, wishing it was whiskey. He glanced at his watch. Madelaine's charter plane was due in from Fairbanks any time now, and as far as he was concerned, it couldn't land any too soon. The quicker he got this unhappy scene over with, the better for both of them.

At least it would be better for *him*, he acknowledged ruefully. He didn't really know how Madelaine was going to feel about it, but surely, once she gave it some more thought, the sensible, practical side of her nature would see the wisdom of his decision. No matter how friendly and close they'd become through the mail over the past several months, pen pals just didn't up and get married without actually meeting each other—unless they were crazy.

Jeremy winced as he recalled his state of mind during his first Alaskan winter, all alone in an isolated fishing lodge, a hundred miles from nowhere. "Crazy" was putting it mildly. With no one but himself to talk to for weeks on end, he'd suffered from the ridiculous delusion that he was in desperate need of a wife.

To that end he'd done what countless other desperate men in the Alaskan bush have done throughout history: placed an ad in the lovelorn column of a paper that circulates in the lower forty-eight states. The half ton of hilarious responses he'd gotten from that single ad had provided him with countless hours of entertainment but no likely prospects—until he'd received a letter from a guileless young woman who lived with her maternal grandparents on a small dairy farm in Iowa.

The loneliness and vulnerability he'd sensed behind the words in Madelaine's introductory letter had struck a responsive chord in him, and without realizing what he was getting into, he'd written back to her. Her reply had been immediate, absolutely charming and surprisingly witty.

Come to think of it, Jeremy hadn't wasted much time getting back to her, either. And that had been the start of their long-distance affair. Soon the letters had been flying back and forth between them, often crossing themselves in the mail as they discovered more and more shared interests. Eventually they'd begun pouring their hearts out to one another, and Jeremy had found himself living for Madelaine's letters.

Those letters had been the sunshine that had helped him endure his first Arctic night—a three-month period of time when staying warm had been his prime objective. In a silence as cold and terrifying as the subzero temperatures, he'd swiftly come to adore the noise of a chain saw, the hiss of water boiling over on the hot stove, and the crackle of burning wood in the fireplace. He'd even taken some comfort in the lonely howl of a hungry wolf, for that hair-raising sound had confirmed that he wasn't completely alone in the world.

Preparing and eating meals became the highlight of Jeremy's day, and as the unrelenting darkness continued, he'd found himself becoming more and more creative with his menus, then savoring each different taste as if his life depended on the culinary success of his complex and oftimes outlandish recipes. Eventually he'd become bored with that nonsensical occupation and had devoted most of his time to reading, but he'd quickly read through the meager supply of books he'd brought with him. Wood carving hadn't turned out to be his specialty, either, and he had several scars left on his fingers to prove it.

For a time he'd enjoyed drawing up renovation plans for the lodge, figuring and refiguring his ideas for future construction, but without anyone with whom to share his ideas, he'd quickly lost his enthusiasm for that, too—until Maddy. Her interest in his plans for Stoney Point had rejuvenated his own, and also satisfied his insatiable need for something—anything—to do that would counterbalance the blandness of a seemingly endless tranquillity. By the end of December, he'd become a prolific letter writer.

As Jeremy remembered some of the more gushy, romantic things he'd written to her, all the personal feelings he'd shared with her and the idealistic plans they'd made together for the future, he felt like a first-class heel. He felt even worse when he thought about the things he'd chosen *not* to tell her in order to preserve the image she had of him as a rough and tough mountain man. He was indeed familiar with life at high altitudes, but only because he'd spent the majority of his adult life inside the tallest New York skyscrapers. Up until a year ago, the roughest and toughest thing he'd ever done, not including that summer during his junior year of high school when he'd worked on a construction crew, was to increase a thousand-dollar investment into a hundred-thousand-dollar profit.

"Oh, Maddy," he murmured sadly, unconsciously savoring the feel of her name on his tongue, just as he'd savored every word she'd written to him over the seemingly interminable winter. "You were such a lifesaver."

But that was then, and this was now. At long last, spring had arrived to thaw out his brain, and he'd regained his lost sanity. Over his thirty-three years as an eligible bachelor, he'd honed his skills in artful dodging to an expert level, and with some very fancy footwork he'd managed to successfully avoid the matrimonial trap. Even if Maddy *did* come across as the perfect woman for him, he still wasn't ready to take that final step into permanent bondage.

Cautiously he tested the sound of a woman's name linked with his. "Madelaine Price Kincaid...Mrs. Jeremy Russel Kincaid."

His mouth went dry over the last title. "Good God. Why did I ever let things progress this far?"

"A little late to be getting cold feet now, ain't it, Jeremy?" Big Sal asked out of the side of her generous mouth as she plunked her ample girth down next to him at the table. Without dislodging a speck of a lengthy gray ash that dangled from the end of her cigarette, she advised, "Best you remember that some of these boys drove their rigs all night long just so's they wouldn't miss out on the ceremony. They've been known to get a mite rowdy when they're riled."

Jeremy held up one hand before matchmaker Sal, the treacherous female who'd first planted the idea of advertising for a mate in his snow-clogged brain, really got started on him. "If they do, it won't be my fault," he grumbled, digging his fingers through the springy dark hairs of his newly trimmed beard. "You're the one who invited them. I don't even *know* half of these people."

"I didn't invite nobody," Sal vehemently denied. "Ever since I convinced you to put that ad in the paper, these boys have been checkin' in with me to see if anything came of your mail-order romance. It's not *my* fault that something did."

"True," Jeremy allowed miserably, but then a comforting thought came to him, and his brown eyes regained some of their lost sparkle. "Hey! Even if I don't go through with the wedding, most of the guys won't blame me for a wasted trip. The way I hear it, all the smart money's on my backing out."

"Well, I've matched every one of those bets, Kincaid, so I'll be out a real bundle if you disappoint me," Sal warned tartly.

"Great," Jeremy growled. "That's just great."

Sal ignored the sarcasm, her lined face splitting into a wide grin as she heard the sound of an airplane circling overhead. Slapping Jeremy on the shoulder, she stood up and announced jovially, "Better finish off your beers, boys, and ante up your money, 'cuz here comes the bride!"

"Oh, God," Jeremy groaned. But he was the first man out of his chair and the first one out the door as the boisterous crowd headed toward the airstrip.

All eyes were on the hatch of the plane as it opened and the metal ramp was let down. Then, as a tall slender blonde wearing a pretty blue shirtwaist dress with a cinched waist and low-heeled shoes made her appearance, a collective gasp could be heard. A brisk wind was blowing as she started descending the steps, her skirt flew up above her knees, showing off a pair of long, curvy legs that were tanned to perfection.

"We're talking great gams, here, Kincaid," Fred Simpson, an exploration geologist, declared enthusiastically. "And the rest of her ain't bad, either."

Boyd Mason, a barrel-chested trucker who hauled freight down from Coldfoot was equally impressed. "Nice set of headlights, too. Real nice."

Boyd's partner, Dillon Pike, whistled his appreciation, and the wolfish tune was immediately picked up by several other of the men. Jeremy would have told them to knock it off if he could have, but since he felt as if he'd just been punched in the stomach, he was helpless to do anything but stand by in paralyzed silence as his "fiancée" stepped onto the tarmac.

Pictures often lied, so he'd geared himself up for a disappointment, but the snapshot he'd been mooning over for the past six months didn't do justice to the real woman. If looks were anything to go by, Madelaine Price was not only a sexy, blond bombshell, but according to her flushed cheeks, she was as unaffected and wholesome as she'd sounded in her letters. And just like all the other men in the crowd, Jeremy found himself gaping at her like an adolescent.

She was beautiful. Her shoulder-length curly hair was the pale color of corn silk, and it tumbled wildly around a face that was lightly tanned but absolutely free of any artifice. Unlike most modern women, she'd done nothing to hide the delightful sprinkle of freckles over her nose, and the rosy color in her cheeks was as natural as the soft pink of her lips. Just as in her picture, her eyes were big and blue, and her gaze was disarmingly direct.

As if she'd known him forever, she picked him out in the crowd and walked right up to him. "Hello, Jeremy," she said shyly, in the same voice he'd chosen for her in his dreams—a soft, low, husky voice.

"Er...hello," he stuttered, forcing his eyes away from that fabulous body, which was better than anything he'd imagined in any of his erotic fantasies. One whale of a lot better!

"It's so good to finally be here," she said, smiling at him conspiratorially, mistakenly assuming that the shyness she suffered was one of the many traits they had in common. Painfully aware that she was the center of attention, her cheeks were on fire, but there was only a slight catch in her voice as she continued, "I didn't realize what a truly long way it is from Iowa to Alaska."

"Uh-huh," Jeremy mumbled stupidly, as she held out her hand to him in friendly greeting.

Jeremy ordered his hand to emerge from his pants pocket, his fascinated gaze on the impish grin he saw peeping around the two enchanting dimples in her cheeks. "Are you as terrified and nervous as I am?" she asked softly.

Jeremy nodded his head up and down, and he grasped her hand because he desperately needed something to hang on to. In a daze, he registered the fact that her fingers were strong and her palm slightly rough, as if she were used to hard work. Of course, she'd told him that in her letters, but he'd talked himself out of believing it, just as he'd talked himself out of believing that his ideal woman existed. Yet, here she was in the flesh, speaking to him in her ideal-woman voice and smiling her ideal-woman smile. And that body.... Oh, Lord...that magnificent ideal-woman body.

"Jeremy?"

"Maddy," he croaked, unable to stop himself from grinning back at her as he pumped vigorously on her hand.

"You were right. This *is* the hard part," she managed breathlessly, reminding him of what he'd said to her in his last letter—that damnable letter wherein he'd described the arrangements he'd made for their wedding and enclosed the tickets for her flight to Alaska. "We're bound to feel awkward at first, but everything is going to work out okay. All we've got to do is remember that we both want the same thing."

"Right," Jeremy muttered, as he gazed bemusedly into her expressive blue eyes.

"We're friends first," she whispered expectantly.

But he couldn't get the words he felt she was looking for past the huge lump in his throat. He remembered them, though, and wished heartily that he'd
never put them down on paper. *Lovers can wait until
later. I promise we won't sleep together until we're
both ready.* He didn't know about Maddy, but he was
ready right now.

"Friends," he finally managed, and was rewarded
by a relieved smile that turned his insides to warm
mush.

For several moments they just stood there, making
cow eyes at each other, completely unaware of those
around them until Big Sal stepped forward to get the
ball rolling again. After introducing herself, she
grasped Madelaine by the shoulders and led her away
from her shell-shocked intended. "C'mon honey.
Time's a-wasting. Reverend Murdock has a funeral to
attend down in Fairbanks, so as soon as this plane gets
gassed up, he'll be taking off. You and Jeremy can do
all your talking once you get back to your own place.
Hell, you'll have years and years to talk, once you've
tied the knot."

Sal's use of that particular terminology knocked
Jeremy out of his dumbfounded stupor, and his hand
jerked up to the collar of his white dress shirt as if he
could feel a noose tightening around his throat.
"Maddy!" he shouted in desperation, but the crowd
of onlookers had closed ranks around Big Sal and her
overwhelmed charge, and Jeremy couldn't break
through to them without breaking a few very large,
masculine bones.

"Dammit to hell," he swore in frustration, as the
two self-appointed groomsmen took hold of his arms
and helped him along to the preacher.

"It could be worse, Kincaid," Boyd Mason advised, noting Jeremy's sickly color. "She could've been as homely as a mud fence."

Dillon Pike sought to help by delivering a weather report. "The Almanac says we're in for another real bad winter, but it won't be that bad for you if you're snowed in with the likes of her."

"I'm too young to get married," Jeremy complained, which made the other two men bark with laughter.

"I was only eighteen when they put the shackles on me," Boyd recalled, directing a pointed glance to his partner. "Prison life ain't easy, but you'll get used to it."

Dillon added his dubious encouragement. "I've been linked up to my ball and chain for twenty years now. And all things considered, it ain't so bad. I get fed on a fairly regular basis and she makes sure my shirts stay pretty clean."

Jeremy shook his head in growing despair as Boyd grinned.

"And after a few years, you'll be so busy chasing after a slew of runny-nosed kids, you won't have time for second thoughts. Why, I've got so many of them little beggars running around home, I can barely think straight."

"That's why we signed up for these long hauls," Dillon agreed. "Married or not, a man needs some time alone."

Jeremy's footsteps were really dragging by the time they arrived at Sal's doorstep, but the eagle-eyed woman was right there waiting for him. She took one look at his grinning escorts and let loose with a blast of curses that would singe the ears off a grizzly. "I

should have known you two fly-by-nights would try
and pull something like this. Just because you boys
stand to lose a week's salary don't give you the right
to break that young gal's heart. Jeremy made that
sweet thing a promise of his own free will, and whatever horror stories you've told him, he's got way too
much honor to go back on his word. Don't you, Jeremy?''

Jeremy didn't care for the way Sal had posed that
question, but he didn't have to worry about coming up
with a noncommittal answer. Sal acted on the assumption that it would be "Yes," and hauled him
unceremoniously through the door. The next thing he
knew, he was standing in front of Reverend Murdock, and the fast-talking preacher was asking him if
he would take Madelaine Elizabeth Price as his law-
fully wedded wife.

He was about to say no, but then he made the mistake of looking Maddy's way, and it was all over for
him. A surge of protectiveness rose up inside him as he
saw the vulnerability on her face and the nervous plea
in her big blue eyes—such a strong surge of tender-
ness that his mouth formed the words with no help
from his brain: "I . . . do."

Maddy's face paled to the color of chalk when
Reverend Murdock posed the same question to her.
Thinking she was about to faint, Jeremy took hold of
her arm, but there was no hesitation in her voice as she
said the words, and the tremulous smile she gave him
made his heart turn over. Whatever happened, no
matter how strange their courtship and marriage, this
sweet, innocent woman trusted him to make things
right, and God help him, Jeremy found himself praying that he had the power to do so.

When Reverend Murdock asked for the ring, Jeremy produced the simple gold band he'd purchased for the occasion, and slipped it onto Maddy's trembling finger, just for the chance of holding her hand. "With this ring, I thee wed," he repeated dutifully after the preacher, and with those words, he sealed his fate and hers.

Five minutes later, as he pressed a brief kiss on her soft mouth, Jeremy realized that he'd done so with nary a protest. For reasons he still couldn't fathom, he'd just promised to have and to hold Madelaine Price from this day forward in the bonds of holy matrimony. And he was a man of his word. Luckily, his wife seemed almost as stunned by her new status as he was, and therefore didn't question his lack of enthusiasm as Big Sal offered them her congratulations, then called for the celebration to begin.

The next two hours went by in a blur. Vaguely Jeremy was aware that he and Maddy were seated together in a vinyl-covered booth, that they were given something to eat and to drink, and were toasted numerous times before the crowd lost interest in them. He understood that Big Sal was thrilled by the amount of money she raked in when all the losers paid up, but other than that, he wasn't conscious of anything except the nauseating stream of platitudes running through his mind.

It was all over now, but the shouting.

The die had been cast.

He'd made his bed, now he could lie in it.

Marry in haste, repent at leisure.

"A penny for your thoughts?"

Jeremy scowled. Now why would he ask himself a stupid question like that? He knew exactly what he was thinking and none of his thoughts were worth a tinker's damn. He was doomed—doomed!

"Jeremy?" Maddy inquired, when he didn't answer her. "Is something wrong?"

"Huh?" Jeremy lost the grip on the handle of his beer mug when he realized who was talking to him. As he stumbled to right the teetering glass, he suddenly became aware of all the bad language, dense smoke and raunchy smells that typified any visit to Big Sal's. "Wrong? Nothing's wrong," he groaned. "Not a thing. Nope."

Maddy shocked him into silence by placing her hand soothingly over his clenched fist and smiling indulgently. "You don't have to be uptight around me, Jeremy. After living alone for so long, you probably don't feel comfortable in such a crowded setting, but these people are your friends, and I'm sure they mean well."

Maddy was operating under the misguided notion that Jeremy was a bashful hermit, a simple man who lacked social skills. Since he had thoroughly enjoyed her erroneous assumption, he hadn't combated it. But now he felt guilty for having deceived her, especially since she was being so blasted kind. "Yeah, I'm sure they do," he conceded gruffly, accepting the growing ache in his head that was the perfect accompaniment to his sick stomach. "But I wouldn't really call them friends. I know Big Sal pretty well, but I've only seen the rest of these guys a time or two."

Maddy's feather-light brows drew together as she glanced around the crowded diner. "If they barely know you, why would they come to your wedding?"

Jeremy cleared his throat anxiously and shifted uncomfortably in his seat, but when she gazed at him with those huge blue eyes of hers, he couldn't lie. "Big Sal has a big mouth, and as soon as she heard I was getting married, she passed the news on to every trucker who stopped in. Since she also happened to tell them how our relationship got started, most of these boys were willing to bet that I'd back out before the wedding."

Jeremy could feel the tips of his ears turning red as he forced himself to say the rest. "Unbeknownst to me, Big Sal took on all their bets, and she was laying some pretty high odds that I'd stick to my word. These guys were positive that she'd lose, and they showed up to claim their money."

"I see," Maddy replied.

"Life can get pretty boring up here," Jeremy explained apologetically.

"So you said in your letters."

Jeremy nodded. But that concession didn't make him feel less uncomfortable. A woman deserved much better than this on her wedding day—and he knew it. They both knew it. "I'm sorry, Maddy. I didn't plan this thing out very well. I should have come down to Fairbanks for the wedding, instead of asking you to come up here."

To his astonishment, Maddy burst out laughing— not with the tight, stilted laughter of embarrassment, but with uncontrollable giggles of sheer delight. Blue eyes twinkling, she glanced over at the ancient juke-box blaring out-of-date music, then around at the huge stuffed-animal trophies staring back at her from the walls. When she heard Big Sal, standing behind the bar, turning the air blue with one of her off-color jokes, Maddy laughed all the harder.

For a few seconds Jeremy feared she was becoming hysterical, but then she leaned over toward him and gave him an exuberant hug. "I wasn't expecting hearts and flowers, Jeremy, but this . . . This . . ."

Words failed her as she doubled over at the table, clutching her stomach and laughing until the tears rolled down her cheeks. Nonplussed, Jeremy stared at her, trying and failing to think of one woman in his considerable acquaintance who would have responded to this ridiculous farce in the way Maddy was. He would have expected tears, but not of this kind. If she'd screamed at him like a banshee or started throwing things, he would have understood, but he didn't comprehend this reaction at all. She was acting as if she were having the best time of her life.

It took several moments for her to regain control of herself, but when she finally did, she lifted her beer mug, took a huge swallow, then swiped the foam off her mouth with the back of her hand. "You dear, sweet man," she complimented, bestowing a beaming smile at him. "You have nothing to apologize for. A woman's wedding day is supposed to be the most memorable day in her life, and you've certainly succeeded there beyond my wildest dreams. I'll never forget this amazing day as long as I live!"

Jeremy's brows rose at least an inch. "You're not upset?"

"Not at all," Maddy assured him, as she took a big bite of the mooseburger that had heretofore remained untouched on her plate. "This is your world, Mr. Kincaid, and I just agreed to share it of my own free will. I'll admit it's going to take some getting used to, but as I've already told you, I'm game if you are."

Jeremy stared at her consideringly, still disbelieving. No woman was this accommodating. For the first time, he wondered if his sweet, guileless Madelaine had chosen to leave out as much important information about herself in their correspondence as he'd neglected to tell *her*. "This place is on the far edge of my world, Maddy," he informed her bluntly. "Compared to Stoney Point, this is civilization."

Once again he was taken aback by her reaction: "I see," she murmured thoughtfully, then grinned. "Well, then, I don't know about you, Mr. Kincaid, but I can't wait to leave civilization behind and start for home."

Neither could Jeremy. But he was sure Maddy didn't fully understand how drastically rustic "rustic" could be. "That's because you've never been there before, and I...I may have exaggerated a bit in my letters," he admitted. "My—our place is beautiful, but it will take some work to make it more livable. As long as the big ones are biting, fishermen don't notice the lack of amenities, but believe me, you will."

Maddy pooh-poohed his concern. "I won't mind roughing it, and I can't wait to get there. How far do we have to go?"

"As the crow flies, about ninety miles, but you've already put in a long day." With an unconsciously wistful sigh, he offered her another out. "I thought we could stay here for the night, and start out after breakfast in the morning. That way, you can get a decent night's sleep before you have to put up with a sagging mattress, cold water and outdoor plumbing."

Employing one of his favorite phrases, Maddy swiftly negated that idea. "No way. I've already waited six months, I don't think I can wait another minute, let alone another day.''

Jeremy shook his head at her animated expression and the naive enthusiasm of her tone, wondering how long it would take to change her tune once reality set in. According to his letters, Stoney Point was a wilderness paradise, a place where the human spirit was confined only by the bounds of nature. But he didn't think Maddy quite realized what it took to survive in such a place. When she found out the true meaning of *primitive*, their marriage would probably turn out to be one of the shortest on record.

Considering that intriguing possibility, Jeremy conjured up some very real enthusiasm of his own. If she was the one who wanted out, he wouldn't have anything to feel guilty about, and they might even be able to part friends. Sliding quickly out of the booth, he declared brightly, ''Then let's get our goodbyes over with, and head out to the plane.''

''I'm right behind you,'' Maddy said, grabbing hold of his hand as Jeremy marched purposefully toward the bar.

Two

***

Off *we go into the wild blue yonder,* Maddy murmured to herself, holding on to the edge of her seat for dear life as the lightweight Cessna lifted smoothly off the ground, gained altitude, then veered sharply toward the distant mountains. Trying to conquer her unexpected attack of nerves, she directed her gaze to the large, competent hands of her pilot who was manning the controls. Unfortunately, as soon as she looked over at Jeremy, she remembered that he was not only her pilot, but her husband.

Taking a deep breath, Maddy resigned herself to her fate. There was no getting around it. She'd just taken an irrevocable step and it was too late to turn back. She had married a man she knew only through his letters, and now he was taking her home with him to begin their life of wedded bliss. As daunting as she found that prospect, Maddy forced herself to remain calm and remember all the logical reasons she'd had for doing something this crazy in the first place.

She just had to keep telling herself that though she'd never actually met Jeremy before today, he wasn't really a stranger. He was a friend—a good friend. Over the past several months, she'd learned all there was to know about him, even if she hadn't found out anything in person.

Therefore she had absolutely no reason to worry. None.

From everything she'd seen thus far, Jeremy was indeed the same shy, sweet, old-fashioned man she'd befriended through the mail—exactly the kind of man her grandparents had always wanted for her. Which was another reason she'd accepted Jeremy's proposal. Marriage to Jeremy meant that she would no longer have to see the worry and disappointment in her grandparents' eyes whenever they looked at her. Though they'd never come right out and said so, the old couple considered her a quitter—a flighty, unstable woman who wasn't capable of settling down. Unfortunately she'd given them good reason to think so.

With or without family approval, however, Maddy would have been tempted to accept Jeremy's offer to join him in Alaska. After so many years of living in a plastic, big-city world filled with plastic, big-city people, she was totally enamored of the kind of life-style Jeremy had described in his wonderful letters: a simple, yet productive life in a beautiful, untouched place where independence and individuality were respected, not scorned. Beyond that, she had always yearned for a marriage that would last, which meant finding a man of sterling character, a man who shared her values, a man she could trust.

From all indications, Jeremy Kincaid was that man.

Then why was she so frightened? Maddy got her answer to that question every time she dared to glance at her new husband's face. She'd learned from harsh experience not to trust handsome men; and beneath his full beard, Jeremy Kincaid was gorgeous, much better looking than he'd appeared in that picture he'd sent to her. Maybe if she'd studied the big burly man in that snapshot more closely, she would have noticed the roguish features hidden behind those scraggly whiskers, and the drop-dead masculine body contained inside that fur-lined parka.

And those eyes! Deep, dark, bedroom eyes—eyes that matched his strong, chiseled jaw and sensual mouth.

Why hadn't she noticed all that about him when she'd had the chance? Because at the time she'd received the picture, she'd had no interest in his looks, that's why. Back then, her sole concern had been for the inner man. But now, Maddy realized that Jeremy Kincaid possessed a face and body that would turn any woman's head, including her own.

But he doesn't know it, Maddy reminded herself. Which makes him even more special. Please, God, let me be right about him. Please let this work out, she prayed fervently, insecure as she was in her own judgment about men and relationships, and unaware that her face reflected her anxiety.

"Scared?" Jeremy inquired, the rich tenor of his voice setting off explosive flutters in her stomach—the kind of flutters a woman suffered when she began to wonder what it would feel like to make love with a man. In fact she'd been thinking about that aspect of their marriage practically nonstop ever since the ceremony. It was just that she hadn't expected Jeremy to be so... so thrillingly male; and it was mind-boggling to think that she would be the one to show him what he could do with all that untapped virility.

Oh, Lord! Maddy squeezed her eyes shut. *What if he was a virgin!*

"Maddy? Are you okay?"

"Of course, I'm okay," she choked out, trying desperately to get a handle on her intense attraction to a man who could very well run in the opposite direction at the mere mention of the word *lust*. If he was as modest as she suspected, she was just going to have to be patient and keep her hands off him. But all he had to do was look at her, and her toes curled.

Her reaction to him shocked her. Up until now, she'd never considered Jeremy in any other light than as her dear friend and confidant. After their marriage, she'd imagined the physical side of their relationship to develop slowly over time and that eventually, it would settle down into a nice, comfortable pattern. But she wasn't feeling very comfortable at the moment, and *nice* was the last word she would use to describe her astonishingly graphic thoughts.

"You're sure?" Jeremy asked skeptically.

"Positive."

"Then why don't you let go of that death grip you've taken on your seat," Jeremy advised. "I happen to be an excellent pilot."

Maddy's gaze darted to his mouth and the telltale twitch around his lips. Was Jeremy Kincaid laughing at her? Jeremy, a man who had so little confidence in his ability to attract a woman that he'd resorted to placing an ad in a lovelorn column? Intending to find out, Maddy recited the facts that she'd been given in one of his most recent letters. "I'm aware of that. You started taking flying lessons at fourteen and got your private's license the minute you turned eighteen. Why, you could probably set this baby down safely on a silver dollar."

A tinge of red came up on the back of Jeremy's neck. "I guess that must have sounded like I was bragging, huh?"

Maddy's dimples came out to tease him, though her smile was as gentle and soothing as her voice. He was such a dear, unassuming man. "That's okay. Unlike me, you can do something that's really worth bragging about."

"That's not true. You're a woman of many talents."

"Oh?" Maddy inquired, and after that next comment, she was the one who was left with a disconcerted flush on her cheeks.

"Yes, 'Oh,'" Jeremy declared emphatically. "You know how to milk a cow by hand, bake homemade bread and can vegetables. You can also make your own clothes and cut your own hair. You can catch and clean fish as well as any angler. In fact, if I get laid up for some reason and can't go hunting, you can shoot a rifle with the best of them. Not to mention your considerable experience with a hammer and saw."

Maddy squirmed guiltily as she recalled how many years it had been since she'd actually done any one of those things. "Speaking of bragging..."

Jeremy grinned at her discomfort. "C'mon. Don't sell those abilities short. Where we're going, those kinds of skills are invaluable. I wasn't lying when I told you that getting involved with me meant stepping back in time to the pioneer days."

"Yes...well..." Maddy's voice trailed off as it occurred to her that for a man who had been isolated from society for most of his life, Jeremy was having very little trouble conversing. Then, as she compared the facts she knew about him with what she *didn't* know, she realized that she might have only assumed he'd spent his entire life in the wilds. What if he hadn't? She stared suspiciously at him.

Jeremy sensed the change in her mood and frowned. "Is something wrong?"

"To tell you the truth," Maddy admitted frankly, "I wasn't expecting you to hold up your end of the conversation like this."

"Why not?"

Hoping to inspire another blush, which would do wonders for her peace of mind, Maddy stated bluntly, "Because you're painfully shy. You don't have much experience around women, and therefore I make you very nervous."

To her dismay, his face didn't change color. "Where did you get that crazy idea?" Jeremy asked with surprise. "I never told you anything like that in my letters."

"You didn't have to tell me. Since it took weeks for you to work up the courage to write anything personal, and another month to say anything that could be considered the least bit romantic, it seemed perfectly logical to make those assumptions."

"You know what they say about people who make assumptions," Jeremy said with a grin—an arrogant, conceited, man-about-town grin.

Seeing it, Maddy's sense of unease grew to major proportions. "Well, you certainly didn't do anything to change my opinion of you before now," she accused. "When you saw me step off that plane, you blushed to the roots of your hair, and you could barely talk when I introduced myself to you."

"You weren't exactly what I was expecting, either," Jeremy came back defensively. "It took me a while to recover my equilibrium."

Postponing the questions that this amazing admission inspired, Maddy continued pressing him. "Sorry, but I didn't notice much improvement in your country-bumpkin routine at the wedding."

When deliberately provoked, Jeremy didn't think twice about fighting back or fighting dirty. "You might be an Iowan hayseed, lady, but I'm no 'country bumpkin.' I happen to hail from New York."

Maddy's mouth dropped. "New York? You're from New York!"

Jeremy found her incredulity just short of insulting. "As a matter of fact," he declared, "I only moved to Alaska last year. Before that, I was an account executive on Wall Street."

Finding no change in her blank, disbelieving expression, Jeremy elaborated in a tone that questioned her intelligence. "You know—a stockbroker, one of those wheeler-dealer types who drink three-martini lunches and always travel in the fast lane?"

Maddy stared at him as if he'd suddenly turned into a monster. "Then . . . then all that hemming and hawing around was just an act?"

"Hemming and hawing!" Jeremy burst out indignantly. "Reverend Murdock talked so fast I didn't get the chance to think, let alone back out."

"'Back out'!" Maddy cried, as if she were hit below the belt again. "You wanted to back out on *me*?"

Considering her less-than-gratifying opinion of him, and the inflated one she had of herself, Jeremy wasn't about to tell her why he'd gone ahead with their marriage. She might be gorgeous, but she was holy hell on the ego, and he was happy to have the chance to poke a few pricks in her self-centered balloon. "Since I've enjoyed my pick of beautiful women for several years now, the thought *did* cross my mind that you wouldn't come up to my usual standards. But then I saw that if you put on some makeup, you wouldn't be half bad-looking, and I decided, what the heck? A man gets mighty lonely up here, and none of the women I know would come within a hundred miles of my place."

"Oh, my God," Maddy breathed, as all of her idyllic *Little House on the Prairie* dreams went up in a cloud of smoke. This man wasn't a modern version of Pa Wilder—a man of honor and integrity. This man was a low-down, conniving snake in the grass.

Jeremy glared at her. If she hadn't lit the short fuse of his temper, he wouldn't have gotten sarcastic. But now that the damage was done, he wanted her to admit that this situation was as much her fault as his. "Don't tell me you didn't suffer a moment's doubt."

Ignoring that pertinent question, Maddy sighed miserably. "And I thought I knew you so well."

"We *do* know each other," Jeremy barked impatiently. "Just not well enough to get married."

"You lied to me, made me think you were some kind of backwoods hermit."

Jeremy stiffened at her accusation. "Maybe I'm guilty of a few omissions, but that doesn't make me a liar. And I've never claimed to be a hermit...just a man who likes his privacy."

Speaking more to herself than to him, Maddy moaned, "I thought we were going to be such good friends, the best of buddies."

Disliking the limp category in which she'd placed their relationship, especially since all he could think about was getting her into his bed, Jeremy insisted, "Even you'll have to admit that a good marriage is based on more than friendship. What about passion? What about love?"

"What about honesty and integrity?" Maddy retorted.

Caught in his own trap, Jeremy surrendered. "Okay, those things are important, too."

"So important that you left out half your life in your letters to me."

"You were so hell-bent on believing that I was part man and part grizzly that I didn't want to disappoint you," Jeremy defended himself. "I realize you were operating under a few delusions, and that's why I decided not to go through with this arrangement."

"But you *did* go through with it," Maddy reminded him, before laying her swimming head back on the seat and closing her eyes. Unfortunately she couldn't shut out the strident voice inside her head. It kept telling her that Jeremy Kincaid was just like all the other men in her past: a selfish, arrogant bastard who saw something he liked and took it without care for the consequences.

"You went through with it," she repeated caustically. "And now we're legally married."

Thoroughly annoyed by her holier-than-thou attitude, Jeremy ground out, "If you recall, *Mrs.* Kincaid, my signature wasn't the only one on that marriage certificate.''

''I signed my own death warrant,'' Maddy groaned under her breath.

Jeremy looked over at her deflated form and nauseated expression and got angry all over again. ''If you feel that way about it, we can always get a divorce.''

If anything, his suggestion made her look even sicker. ''This marriage is forever,'' she murmured wretchedly, and gazed over at him, her big blue eyes brimming.

Jeremy opened his mouth to deliver his scathing opinion on that Victorian philosophy, but her tears stopped him. Madelaine Price had been a surprise from the first moment she'd stepped off the plane, but the emotions she inspired in him came as a disturbing shock. As much as he wanted to strangle her, he also wanted to soothe and protect. There was a vulnerability about her that called out to him in a way that he'd never experienced before with a woman, that made him long to take her into his arms and hold her—just hold her until that haunting sadness disappeared from her eyes.

Then it dawned on him that her archaic belief in the sanctity of marriage had been specific rather than general. She hadn't said all marriages were forever; she'd said *this* one was. With his eyes narrowed suspiciously on her pale face, he asked, ''Can I take that to mean you've been married before?''

After a tense pause, Maddy finally gave him an answer. ''Almost,'' she declared bitterly.

''You were engaged to somebody?''

Maddy released a long, shuddering sigh. ''Two somebodies,'' she admitted, shooting him with a kill-ing glare. "One of them was a famous photographer, and the other was one of those wheeler-dealer types who travels in the fast lane."

"Oh." Jeremy swallowed hard at that telling piece of information.

"Yes, 'Oh,'" Maddy returned snidely.

According to the expression on her face, Jeremy realized that she'd already removed him from the "friend" category and had banished him to a far less pleasant place in her mind. Unfortunately he still had a few questions that demanded answers. "What were a famous photographer and a wheeler-dealer doing out in the Corn Belt?"

"That's not where I met them."

"Then where did you?"

Maddy's shoulders sagged as she reluctantly revealed an omission of her own, but one that she'd made to be kind. Not wanting to intimidate him with her supposed "sophistication," she'd let him believe that she'd never left the farm. "I lived in New York for a few years myself."

Every warning sensor in Jeremy's body went off, telling him that he didn't really want to know. But he asked anyway. "Oh? Doing what?"

"I was a model."

"You were a model," Jeremy repeated, in a tone that raised the gooseflesh on Maddy's arms.

"That's right," she said, her eyes going very wide as she watched his knuckles turn white on the controls. And then he turned his head toward her, and his expression was so violent that Maddy would have done anything to get her hands on a parachute.

"A successful model?" he inquired challengingly, as if by the looks of her he couldn't believe anyone in their right mind would hire her.

With a defiant tilt to her chin, Maddy affirmed, "*Very* successful. I've been representing a large cosmetics firm for the past five years. I'm the face they chose to advertise their Dew Drop line of makeup."

Jeremy immediately recognized the name, and he also remembered the huge jump in price of the company's stock when they'd launched their Dew Drop products. Three years ago, the word on the street had been that the management had located such a stunning beauty to pitch the new line that their sales had gone up dramatically within days after the first ad had appeared on television. Jeremy had seen one or two of their glamorous commercials himself, and now he wanted to kick himself for not recognizing the woman who was considered one of the darlings of the cosmetics industry.

"And you had the gall to accuse *me* of putting on an act?" he growled in a tone that could freeze metal. "I thought I was marrying a hardworking, practical farm girl, not some nine-by-twelve color glossy of a real woman."

"I *am* a real woman!" Maddy exclaimed, hating the stereotype that had hung like an albatross around her neck from the day she'd posed for her first photo session. "A hardworking, practical woman who knows more about survival than any namby-pamby desk jockey."

A subject that neither of them had ever discussed in their letters was their short fuses, and Jeremy's temper had swiftly risen to flash point. If she wanted to resort to name-calling, he was more than ready to oblige her. "Baloney! You're nothing but a useless piece of Madison Avenue fluff!"

Her own volatile temper equally aroused, Maddy retorted, "Well, you're nothing but a worthless Wall Street money changer."

"What the hell good are you going to be to me out here in the bush? A model, for God's sake! A know-nothing do-nothing bubble head," Jeremy charged. "You probably don't even sweat. You just get attractively dewy!"

Determined to hold her own in a situation that was rapidly escalating into a full-scale battle, Maddy shot back, "Well, after wallowing around with all those dirty players on the stock market, I'm sure you sweat like a bloody pig."

"I want out of this farce of a marriage. And I want it now!"

"Too bad, buddy! Like I've already told you, I don't believe in divorce!"

Jeremy glared at her, but she didn't even flinch, which told him that she was a force to be reckoned with—a stubborn, highly combustible, feminine force that didn't show any signs of cooling down. She couldn't possibly be serious about this no-divorce business, but now was obviously not the time to fight about it. As angry as he was with her and with the situation, he'd gone through too much today to fare well in an all-out war.

So, if he could somehow manage a strategic retreat, he would come back and fight another day—like tomorrow, the very first thing tomorrow!

To that end, he turned off the automatic pilot and suddenly became very busy at the controls. "We're not done talking about this, Maddy," he warned after several minutes.

"I'm not going anywhere," she replied with cloying sweetness.

"Okay, then," he managed through clenched teeth. "Since we've both been through hell today, what do you say we declare a temporary truce."

"That's fine with me."

"Good. Because we're coming up on the mountains, and if we want to survive until tomorrow, I have to concentrate on where the heck I'm flying," he explained tersely, and pulled back hard on the controls.

More minutes went by—silent minutes that Jeremy didn't find at all peaceful. They were tense with unspoken hostility. And when he couldn't stand the feel of her accusing eyes on him a second longer, he burst out, "Look! If you could stop pouting for a minute, you'd see that you're missing out on a terrific view. Why don't you switch your attention down there to the valley, and you'll be able to see Beaver Lake."

When she immediately complied with that suggestion, Jeremy graciously elaborated on what she was seeing. "Beaver Lake is the first body of water in a series. The largest one is the Big Boreal and it eventually connects up with my...our...my property."

"Our property," Maddy corrected, without looking at him.

Jeremy forced himself to ignore that telling remark and continued with his commentary. "Stoney Point is about fifty miles from here on the south end of the Little Boreal."

One thing Jeremy hadn't lied about was the spectacular scenery, Maddy saw as she gazed wonderingly out the window. The landscape below her was as beautiful as anything she'd imagined in her dreams. Beneath a sweep of craggy, snow-crested peaks that seemed to rim the very top of the world was a wide, seemingly endless valley that housed a chain of several alpine lakes. Linked together by narrow streams of water, they looked like a mismatched necklace of sparkling blue gems. The most distant link in the chain was smaller and narrower than the rest, nestled like a glistening teardrop within the shadowy cleavage of a thick pine-tree covered basin.

Twenty minutes later, Jeremy began a circling descent that brought the details of the wilderness landscape into ever-sharpening focus. On the far shore of the Little Boreal, Maddy could see a bull moose standing in the shallows. Off to the left, she noticed a sudden streak of white motion, and gasped in delight as she recognized a caribou buck on the run. Disturbed by the sound of the approaching plane, a flock of wild geese rose from the lake, their graceful wings crisscrossing the sky.

As Maddy watched their majestic flight, Jeremy leveled off for a smooth-as-silk landing on the water. Once they were down, he glided the plane expertly across the glassy surface in toward shore. He cut the engine, drew in a deep breath and then turned to look at her.

"Better take your shoes off," he advised curtly, before rolling up his pant legs and jumping out into the shallow water.

As Maddy followed his advice, she suddenly became aware of the quiet—an absolute, overwhelming silence. Glancing anxiously out the window at the mountains behind her, she got the strange feeling that those immense black shadows on the horizon would

like to snatch away all the daylight. Of course that
would be impossible, since the sun didn't set for more
than a few hours above the Arctic Circle in the summertime. It had dropped much lower in the sky, however—so low that the mountains obscured its bright
rays and cast long, dark, foreboding shadows over the
mirrorlike surface of the lake.

"I've lost all track of time," Maddy said, feeling a
nervous shiver snake down her spine as Jeremy sloshed
around the plane to her side. "Is it late afternoon or
early evening?"

"It's going on eight," Jeremy informed her as he
helped her down, then bent over to open the hatch and
fetch out her luggage.

Some of the boys at Big Sal's had loaded it into
Jeremy's plane, so this was the first time he'd seen the
number of bags Maddy had brought along. Since
she'd packed practically everything she owned, Maddy
knew that Jeremy wouldn't be able to carry all of it by
himself. She quickly joined him, and grabbed a
shoulder bag and the smallest of her three suitcases.
Before turning her back on him, she heard Jeremy
grunt with exertion as he pulled out the two larger
ones, but he didn't make any comment, and she didn't
ask for one.

Meekly she followed behind him as he sloshed the
short distance to the shore. Once on land, Jeremy
didn't bother to put his shoes back on but waited po-
litely for Maddy to replace hers before they continued
walking.

"Is it very far to the lodge?" she asked, in an attempt to break the uncomfortable silence between
them.

"Not far," Jeremy replied gruffly, setting a brisk pace across the rocky beach. As they headed for a narrow path between the trees, Maddy decided that her husband not only had great legs and nicely developed buttocks, but feet that were tough enough to walk on nails. Even wearing shoes, Maddy had difficulty keeping up with him, but Jeremy was making no concessions for her shorter stride.

"Not exactly as smooth as a Manhattan sidewalk, is it?" he challenged darkly, glancing back to see how far she'd fallen behind. "Need any help with those bags? If they're anything like these two, they probably weigh a ton."

As she picked her way among the jagged stones, Maddy made a silent vow: Jeremy Kincaid might think he was tough, but he was going to find out that she could be tougher. "No thanks," she replied. "They're not that heavy."

"Humph," Jeremy grunted, and continued walking.

The distance to the lodge wasn't long, but the path leading to it was steep, and Maddy was soon out of breath. Just when she thought she couldn't take another step, she sighted the rustic building so affectionately described in all of Jeremy's letters. It was rustic all right, but in Maddy's estimation, it didn't quite qualify as a lodge. In actuality, it was a ramshackle log cabin with an open lean-to resting against one end and a rickety shed attached to the other.

"I told you it wasn't the Ritz," Jeremy warned her, the look on his face daring her to tell him what she actually thought of her new home.

"So you did," Maddy acknowledged with a very bright and very false smile. "And I can't tell you how reassuring that is."

Three

———

Jeremy pushed open the heavy Dutch door to the lodge and allowed Maddy to precede him inside. As she stepped past him, he caught a whiff of her seductive perfume, but he forced himself not to respond to it, and as she walked farther into the room, he refused to show his appreciation of the alluring sway of her hips. Cynically he reminded himself that she got paid big bucks to appear as if she were gliding into a room, and the last skill he required in a wife was a sexy walk. Keeping his eyes firmly fixed on the spruce-planked floor, he set down her suitcases, then straightened and waited expectantly for her horrified reaction. To his amazement, it never came.

"Why, this is charming," Maddy announced in childlike delight, as her curious gaze darted around the rectangular front room, lingering with pleasure on the huge, variegated stone fireplace, the sturdy wooden furniture and the wide windows cut out of the thick log walls. "Rustic, but absolutely charming."

"Very rustic," Jeremy agreed dryly as he pointed through the heavy beamed archway leading to the kitchen and followed her into the room.

Archaic would be a better word for it, Maddy thought in dismay. With an immediate dampening of her enthusiasm, she surveyed the warped wooden counters and cupboards, the cracked, dingy windows and dirty, uneven floor. The stove was the kind of black, wood-burning antique she'd seen pictured in books but had no idea how to use, and the icebox was just that—an old-fashioned wooden cupboard with space to hold a thick chunk of ice.

Making note of Jeremy's I-told-you-so expression, however, she predicted cheerfully, "A little hot water and soap are going to do wonders in here."

Jeremy had to admire her for her acting ability, but he doubted her pretense would hold up for long. Directing her attention to the iron pump set up on the counter nearest the small rust-stained sink, he warned her, "That's as close to running water as we've got. If you want it hot, you'll have to heat it up on the stove."

"No problem," Maddy replied airily, as she walked back into the main room then sauntered down the narrow hallway to the left, opening the first door along the way and peering inside. There wasn't much to look at: only a crude chest of drawers and three empty bunk beds.

"You won't find a bathroom," Jeremy announced, neglecting to mention that the plumbing supplies he'd purchased were due to arrive at the first of the week. With any luck, she would be long gone before they were delivered. "To get to the outhouse you go through that back entrance at the end of the hall. It's about twenty feet behind the lodge, at the bottom of the hill.''

"Uh-huh," Maddy said, overwhelmed by the amount of work it was going to take to get this place ready for the high-paying clientele they were hoping to attract. Despite what Jeremy had said, she was certain most wealthy businessmen weren't going to be happy in such primitive surroundings. They were going to expect much better accommodations.

Jeremy watched her enter another bedroom, then come back out again and proceed to the next. Each time she returned to the hall, her expression became more thoughtful and considering, as if she were mentally tabulating a long list of improvements in her mind. If that was the case, she wasn't expecting to depart anytime soon, which brought a deep scowl to Jeremy's face. Apparently the angry words they'd exchanged on the plane had left little or no impression on her.

Jeremy had already figured out that Maddy had a mulish streak, but surely even she could see that their marriage wasn't going to work out. It had been fun making up all sorts of plans for the future of the lodge, but fun time was over. The reality of the situation was that neither one of them was the person the other thought he or she was.

To Jeremy's way of thinking, that basic truth negated their whole deal.

He'd contracted for a strong, practical woman, an experienced helpmate. Maddy had represented herself as that kind of woman, but now he knew he'd fallen for one of the slickest con games in the book.

She'd suckered him in with the old bait and switch, but he would be damned before he let her get away with it.

"One of the first things we're going to have to do is add on some more bedrooms," Maddy stated briskly, after completing her inspection.

A calculating expression in her eye, she judged, "Six beds to a room is a bit much, especially when you consider the exorbitant price we're intending to charge for just a week's stay. Our guests might not mind bunking in with their friends, but they're not going to like sleeping with strangers."

Gratified by the chance to point out her ignorance, Jeremy forgot all about the vow he'd just taken and retorted, "Then you don't know anything about sports fishermen. As long as they're reeling in trophy-size fish, they won't care where they sleep or how much it costs."

Stepping past her, he opened the door to one of the six sparsely furnished bedrooms and pointed to a cot that was minus any springs or mattress. "I paid two thousand dollars for a week on that thing."

"You're kidding!" Maddy exclaimed, truly shocked.

"Considering the amount of great fish I caught during those seven days, I thought I was getting off cheap. In fact, I enjoyed my vacation so much, I ended up buying the place."

"Just like that?"

"Just like that," Jeremy replied with a snap of his fingers. "As luck would have it, Joe Senungtuk was more than happy to sell out. He's getting on in years, and didn't want the responsibility of keeping up this place for another season. I offered to take it off his hands, then and there, if he agreed to come back this summer and serve as a fishing guide. He's one of the best in the business.''

Maddy shook her head as she finally heard the true story of how Jeremy had acquired the lodge. "Amazing."

Jeremy shrugged. "Not really. I was thoroughly fed up with my job in New York. A man can only use so much money, so I was looking around for something else to do with mine. As soon as I saw this place, I knew I'd found what I was looking for, so I stayed."

"You really are the impetuous type, aren't you?" Maddy inquired with a pitying smile, painfully aware that this trait was also *her* biggest downfall.

Before today, Jeremy had never thought of himself as impulsive, but now he was beginning to wonder if it might not be true. Maybe he *was* the kind of guy who could only tread the straight and narrow for so long before going off the deep end and messing up his entire life. After ten hectic years on Wall Street, he'd wanted out. But how many other burned-out brokers would have headed north to Alaska, bought a run-down fishing lodge and married a pen pal?

"I guess so," he admitted grudgingly, more annoyed with her than ever.

"Amazing," Maddy muttered again. Then her brain switched gears and her blue eyes lit up. Going back to his speech on the low expectations of fishermen, she exclaimed, "If what you say is true about our guests, then we don't have to put on an extra addition right away, and we can use our money to remodel that unbelievable excuse for a kitchen."

Jeremy felt an uncomfortable jolt in his belly as she reminded him that theirs wasn't just a love match: before agreeing to marry him, Maddy had made it clear that she wanted a financial share in the restoration of the lodge. She'd insisted that she be allowed to invest some of her own money in their mutual enterprise. At the time, Jeremy had been so touched by her offer that he'd accepted it without disclosing the fact that he didn't require any extra revenue.

When he'd seen the size of her check, he'd assumed the dear girl had sent him her entire life's savings and, overwhelmed by her trust in him, he'd immediately deposited it into his high-interest bank account in Fairbanks. He supposed that technically since he'd cashed the check and drawn on the account, she could make a case for being his legal partner whether or not their marriage survived. And money-wise, she could probably match his resources for financing a long legal battle.

Unnerved by that possibility, Jeremy hedged. "I'm not sure this is the right time to be thinking about making any changes."

"Of course, it is," Maddy declared purposefully. "I can't possibly cook anything decent without the proper equipment."

Irked by her haughty tone, Jeremy retorted without thinking, "Joe Senungtuk managed quite nicely. With a little practice, I don't see why you can't do the same."

"That's because Joe expected his guests to eat fish seven days a week. I was hoping that the new owners might add a little variety to the menu."

Jeremy had to admit that he'd gotten tired of fish in a hurry during his vacation, and had ended up cooking for himself. But then he realized what he was doing: by going along with this ridiculous conversation, he was acting as if there were some chance that

Maddy would be here long enough to have some say in the direction he took for remodelling—which she would not be. Even so, he was in no mood to start another argument with her, since he'd barely held his own in the last one.

"It's too late in the day to start this," he declared wearily. "Why don't we get you settled in, find ourselves something to eat, then call it a night. I don't know about you, but I'm too tired to make any important decisions."

Maddy was equally tired, but with sunshine streaming through all the windows, she doubted she would ever be able to fall asleep. "Okay," she agreed, but Jeremy saw her dubious expression and read her mind.

"It never seems to bother me, but if you need darkness to sleep, we've got darkness," he told her, as he took hold of her arm and escorted her back to where they'd left her luggage. "All the windows have shutters, and if that's not good enough, you can tape some aluminum foil over the glass."

"That should work," Maddy conceded, wishing it would be just as easy to close the shutters on her brain and make it stop thinking for the night. With or without light, she knew she was going to be wide-awake for many hours to come. Still, there was no reason Jeremy had to stay up with her, especially since he'd already complained about how tired he was.

Grateful for the reprieve, Jeremy picked up her two large suitcases and headed for a rickety set of stairs at the back corner of the room. Maddy hadn't noticed them before and didn't know where they led, but she rehoisted her bag over her shoulder and dutifully followed him.

As soon as they got to the top of the stairs, however, she came to a dead halt and exclaimed, "Oh, no, you don't! It's far too soon for this, Jeremy Kincaid. You promised to give me more time, and I'm holding you to it."

At first Jeremy didn't have a clue what she was blithering about, but then he saw where her wary eyes were focused, and immediately understood. The sleeping loft held only one large bed, and she was assuming they were going to share it. Handed such a golden opportunity, Jeremy couldn't resist goading her just a little, especially since she was making it clear that she had no intention of letting *him* off the hook.

"You're the one who keeps insisting that we're legally married," he pointed out logically, his lips curving upward in a mocking smile. "And married people sleep together. I promised to wait to have *sex*."

Maddy gulped. "But...you.... You never said—I can't possibly stay in this room."

"I spent the entire fall fixing up the loft so it would be all nice and snug and cozy. I even had a new bed shipped in from Fairbanks, and now you tell me you can't possibly stay here?"

"Of course I could stay here...but not if you're planning to— What I mean is, I...I can't stay here if *you*'re staying here, too."

"Who would ever have thought that the sophisticated spokeswoman for a multimillion-dollar corporation would have so much trouble articulating," Jeremy teased, his eyes sparkling with devilish amusement.

"I...I usually don't. It's just that—"

Jeremy raised one hand to forestall further protest, taking perverse pleasure in needling her. "You can stop all that hysterical babbling. I don't intend to sleep here," he informed her, then paused consideringly, his eyes giving her body a deliberate once-over as he amended. "At least, not tonight. But who knows what might happen tomorrow—especially if you decide to continue this farce?"

"I can tell you what will happen," Maddy declared tartly. But Jeremy didn't wait around to hear what else she might have to say. Wearing a huge, self-satisfied grin, he started for the stairs.

When he was halfway down, he called back up to her, "Come to the kitchen when you're ready. I hope you're in the mood for something light, because all I plan to do is heat up some porcupine soup and put together a willow-bud salad."

Hateful man! Maddy thought to herself and wanted to stamp her foot in frustration. However, if she did that, he would probably laugh all the harder, and so she called back, "That sounds just fine."

Unfortunately he recognized the pretense in her tone, and she heard his amused chuckle as he completed his descent. A second later, she realized what she'd just agreed to eat. Surely this was yet another example of his less-than-amusing brand of humor. No one in their right mind would actually eat porcupines or make a salad of willow leaves—would they?

Of course not, she assured herself, and turned away from the stairs to begin her unpacking. She started with her smallest case, which she'd carried onto the airplane with her in case she got stranded somewhere along the way. It contained the cosmetics necessary for her nightly regimen, a change of underwear, her pajamas, a lightweight sweater, and her favorite pair of jeans.

Within moments, she'd exchanged her dress for the sweater and jeans and her low-heeled shoes for a pair of sneakers. Unable to face the contents of her next-largest suitcase, she decided that the rest of her unpacking could wait until morning. Still, she wasn't quite ready to go downstairs and confront Jeremy again, so she wandered around the loft, admiring the patchwork quilt on the double bed, the quaint little stove in the corner, and the knotty-pine paneling on the walls. As soon as she opened the drawers to the tall, cherry highboy, she realized that Jeremy had never intended to share sleeping quarters. The drawers were empty, as was the closet. As sensitive to her feelings as the man who'd written her all those beautiful letters had been, Jeremy had obviously planned to give her time to adjust to their marriage.

Since she hadn't seen any sign that any of the downstairs bedrooms was occupied, she wondered where Jeremy intended to sleep, hoping that his room was far enough away from the loft that she wouldn't feel the slightest temptation to join him in bed. Even if he *had* turned out to be a big-city rotter, she was still strongly attracted to him, and the fact remained that they were indeed married.

Moreover, considering the sensual heat she saw burning in those velvety, dark, bedroom eyes of his, Maddy knew that Jeremy was equally attracted to her. If she didn't accept his offer of divorce in the very near future, their marriage was bound to be consummated, and she shuddered at the very idea of divorce.

No matter how she looked at it, Maddy couldn't see an easy resolution to their problems. This time, she couldn't just throw Jeremy's ring back in his face and walk out on their relationship. This time, she'd committed herself both financially and legally; and in her mind, if not in Jeremy's, engagement rings and wedding bands meant two entirely different things.

Taking a deep breath, Maddy marched to the head of the stairs, but she didn't have to stand there for any length of time convincing herself to descend. A delicious odor assailed her nostrils, and since the only thing she'd eaten all day was the greasy burger in Big Sal's truck stop, she was anxious to find the source of the wonderful smell. As she followed her nose to the kitchen, Jeremy was already serving up two steaming bowlfuls, and she pretended not to notice the hot gleam in his eyes as he studied the fit of her jeans.

"Is that porcupine quills and tree bark I smell?" she inquired, with a mouth-watering expression on her face.

"In the bush, porkies are considered good eating," Jeremy informed her knowledgeably, but Maddy understood his ploy. With that nonanswer, he'd managed not to tell an out-and-out lie, but he still wasn't willing to admit the truth.

Going along with the joke, Maddy declared, "Then bring it on."

"There's a much bigger table in the dining hall," Jeremy announced, pointing to a small round table under a double set of windows. "But since it's only the two of us, I thought we could eat in here."

"Okay." Maddy sat down on one of the two mismatched chairs, hiding her distaste when she saw the leftover crumbs and spills on the table's red-and-white checkered oilcloth. Apparently Jeremy knew a thing or two about cooking, but he didn't have much aptitude for cleaning up after a meal.

Foregoing the urge to remark on that failing, Maddy said, "I didn't notice there was a dining hall. Where is it?"

Jeremy placed two bowls of soup down on the table, then returned from the counter with the salad, before taking the place opposite hers. "The lodge isn't laid out with any particular sort of logic," he explained, pointing to a closed door at the back of the kitchen. "There's another short hall through there that leads to the addition Joe put on a few years back. It has two more rooms: a dining room and another bedroom."

"So *that*'s where you're sleeping!"

Jeremy grinned knowingly through his beard. "Worried about that, were you?"

It was difficult to ignore the sexual challenge in his tone, but Maddy managed by picking up a roll of paper towels and using one to wipe off the lower windowpane. "What a beautiful view!" she exclaimed, once she was able to see through the smeared glass.

Jeremy almost laughed at her hasty change of subject, but after that telling little episode in the loft, he was feeling magnanimous, so he allowed her to get away with it. Maddy might be stubborn, but she did have her weaknesses, and the longer she stuck things out, the more likely he was to find more. "You're going to discover that there aren't any lousy views at Stoney Point, inside or out."

"Oh!" Maddy drew back from the window abruptly, startled by the appearance of a sleek, bright-eyed creature peering in at her from the outside sill. "What is that thing?"

"That's only Earl," Jeremy muttered disinterestedly, and continued eating his soup, as if he had long since grown bored of such unexpected animal visitations.

"'Earl'?"

Looking up from his bowl, Jeremy cleared his throat, and Maddy tried not to laugh as she noticed the pink tinge above his dark beard. "I said *ermine*. We get a lot of them around here, as well as squirrels and porcupine and raccoon."

"Have you given them all names?" Maddy inquired innocently. "Or is Earl the only animal you're on a first-name basis with?"

With a sheepish shrug, Jeremy admitted, "Okay, so I've named quite a few of them. As I've already told you, it can get pretty lonely up here, and there was no one else to talk to."

For the first time since they'd arrived, Maddy felt a resurgence of her old affection for him. Maybe the Jeremy she knew and this Jeremy weren't that different, after all. Her blue eyes twinkling, she swallowed a spoonful of soup, then asked, "Who can I expect to meet next?"

Jeremy hesitated for a moment, but when he saw her dig into her soup with such relish, then swallow a forkful of salad, he decided that he would have plenty of ammunition to fire back at her if she had it in her mind to make fun of him.

"Well, first there's Oscar. He's a mangy brown bear who arrives every couple of days to steal honey from the hive he discovered in an old tree stump out front. Then there's Freddy the raccoon. He showed up in April to check out my kitchen supplies. Egbert the eagle comes by every chance he gets to see if Earl and

Freddy would like to be his dinner, and he's got a couple of hawk friends that I might get around to naming one of these days. I was thinking of Hawthorn and Harold."

"Hmm." Maddy considered thoughtfully. "I think Hillary and Heather might be better."

Staring at her in pleased astonishment, Jeremy scoffed, "Come, now. Heather and Hillary? Have you ever actually seen a hawk? They're not the most feminine of birds."

"True," Maddy agreed. "But I'm certain there are just as many female hawks as male ones. What's wrong with giving them a pretty name?"

Jeremy thought for a second, then conceded, "Not a thing. In fact, I did notice that those two have some very nicely manicured talons, and their sharp beaks do remind me of a few women I know. You're right. They probably *are* female."

Ignoring his unsubtle gibe at her sex, Maddy asked him to tell her about the other types of wildlife she could expect to see on a regular basis, and to her surprise and delight, the rest of the meal was completed in companionable conversation. As she finished the last of her soup, she leaned back in her chair and patted her stomach. "That was the best porcupine I ever ate, and after that scrumptious salad, I plan to gnaw on every yummy willow tree I can find."

Jeremy laughed. "Glad you enjoyed them, but you won't find the same flavor in the bark. Some of the Eskimos scrape off the inner bark to eat, but I've found the scrapings too bitter for my taste."

Disconcerted by his matter-of-fact tone, Maddy asked, "C'mon, Jeremy. You don't really expect me to believe that baloney you gave me about willow buds and porcupines? I'll admit you had me going there for a while, but those little things in the salad were Garbonzo beans, and the meat in that soup was either beef or venison."

"If that's what you want to believe, feel free," Jeremy returned blithely. "But I wasn't teasing. I marinated that porky meat for two days to get it that tender, and the reason those willow buds were so tasty is because I boiled them in salt water and mixed them up with melted caribou fat."

It was too late for Maddy to get sick to her stomach, and besides, Jeremy's soup and salad had been delicious, no matter what kind of strange ingredients he'd used to make them. Still, it was difficult for her to believe that a man who'd only moved to the wilderness within the past year had learned so much about living off the fruits of the land. "Who taught you how to make this weird stuff?"

Jeremy's brows rose at her use of terminology, but he was enjoying himself too much to be insulted. "Joe did," he replied easily. "Even *he* got tired of fish by the end of the season, and out here, every man and woman has to be practical. Willow buds are the first touch of green in the spring, and after a long winter without, the craving for any kind of greenery is strong. As for the porcupine, if they're allowed to overpopulate, they can be terrible pests, so it pays to eat as many as you can."

"I see," Maddy replied, wondering what other flora and fauna she would be expected to consume in the name of practicality. "You haven't devised a delectable recipe for broiled mosquitoes or curried flies, have you?"

"Not yet," Jeremy replied, tongue in cheek. "But since you're supposed to be a better cook than I am, maybe you'll come up with something."

"I'll certainly look into it," Maddy came back in the same tone, and couldn't seem to help herself from returning his engaging grin. For a few seconds they allowed themselves to enjoy each other's company, just as they'd looked forward to doing before they'd had their rose-colored glasses stripped away and gotten to view each other in their true light.

Before the companionable silence was replaced by the other much more disturbing emotions that hovered around them like specters, Maddy asked, "Is Joe here now?"

Jeremy shook his head. "He spent last summer and fall here teaching me the ropes, but he wanted to spend the winter with his family. He's not due back until the first of June. Now that the upkeep of the lodge is no longer his concern, he doesn't feel the need to show up much before our first guests arrive."

"Then we're all by ourselves for another month," Maddy said, suddenly aware that Jeremy's presence took up much more than his fair share of the room. The man wasn't touching her, yet she felt surrounded, threatened by his invasion of her space. "Of course, there'll be the construction crew. How soon will they get here?"

"They're already here," Jeremy replied. But before Maddy could take any solace from that announcement, he added, "For the time being, we're it."

"What do you mean, 'We're it'?" Maddy demanded warily. "What can the two of us expect to accomplish?"

"Whatever we set our minds to," Jeremy drawled. "Eventually."

"Eventually!" Maddy exclaimed. "If you plan for us to do all of this work ourselves, it's going to take us forever!"

Jeremy cocked his head to one side, his gaze speculative. "So? Are you in some kind of rush?"

Maddy opened her mouth, but immediately closed it again as she realized that Jeremy was conducting some sort of test. In their letters, they'd agreed that they didn't want a fast-paced life, but Maddy was beginning to think she'd greatly underestimated the scope of Jeremy's belief in that philosophy.

"I thought you shared my priorities, liked the idea of taking life slow and easy, concentrating on what's important in life," Jeremy prodded when she didn't answer him. "Or was that just another one of your attempts to mislead me?"

"I never misled you about my priorities," Maddy insisted. "I gave up my career because I no longer knew who I was underneath all that glamor, and I was never given the chance to find out. My life was nothing but commercials and layouts and interviews. One of the main reasons I came to Alaska was to get away from all those hectic schedules and deadlines and just take pleasure in being alive. I have to believe that there's more to Madelaine Price than her pretty face."

"I'm sure there is," he allowed, though he didn't look convinced. "And what better way to prove your intelligence than involving yourself in a risky business venture? Maybe you thought you could charm a simple backwoods hermit like Jeremy Kincaid into making Stoney Point a successful vacation resort that caters to the rich and famous."

"Don't be ridiculous!"

"Then why all this rush to get started on construction?" he asked, almost certain that he'd found the perfect means to chase her off. "What we don't finish this year, we can always finish next year, or the year after that. Or we may decide that things are okay just as they are."

"But—"

Jeremy cut her off. "We're not under any deadlines, and we can decide our own schedules."

"Are you saying that all those plans and ideas we exchanged in our letters were just so much talk?" Maddy cried. "Was modernizing the lodge just a pipe dream to you?"

"No," Jeremy said. "I think of making the lodge more habitable, of fishing and hunting for food, planting a garden, enjoying an Arctic sunset, as my chosen way of life—not as my new career. If I had only wanted to switch professions, I certainly would have picked something more lucrative. Unless we turn this place into some kind of showplace, there won't be much profit in it. But I didn't come up here to make money."

"Then why run a business at all?"

"You should know the answer to that," Jeremy told her. "Working at something makes a man feel useful, but it has to be the right kind of work, the kind he needs. I've spent the last ten years working with my head. Now I intend to work with my hands."

"So you want to remodel the lodge yourself."

"I don't just want to, I'm going to," Jeremy stated firmly, confident that it was only a matter of time before his ambitious, know-nothing excuse for a "wife" packed up her Gucci luggage and hightailed it back to civilization.

Maddy thought about everything he'd just said and decided that it made a good deal of sense—at least to Jeremy. She'd been rethinking her priorities for a shorter time than he, so she wasn't exactly sure what it would take to make her completely happy; but she *did* know that she was on the right track. For reasons she had yet to explore, there was something about this place and this man that made her feel the first real enthusiasm she'd experienced in a long time.

"Do you know anything at all about construction?"

"Enough. And what I don't know, I can learn."

After a long, considering pause, Maddy murmured, "Okay."

"Okay what?"

"Okay, we'll do the whole thing ourselves."

Jeremy looked stunned. "We *will*?"

"No matter how long it takes," Maddy vowed firmly, very much aware that he'd been hoping for an entirely different response.

Jeremy dropped his head into his hands. "What did I do to deserve this?" he muttered gruffly, and groaned at the impish response he received to the question.

"You should know the answer to that, Mr. Kincaid. You married me."

Four

Maddy lifted a plate out of the sudsy water, but before she could rinse it in the plastic dish tub set aside for that purpose, Jeremy snatched it out of her hand. Too slippery to hold, the wet plate slid out of his fingers and shattered to pieces on the hardwood floor. "At the rate you're going, we may have to put a new set of dishes at the top of our supply list," Maddy declared calmly. "How many does that make now?"

"Two plates and a cup," Jeremy snapped, as he went down on his haunches to pick up the broken crockery.

"I realize that our verbal agreement is perfectly legal, but if I'd known you were going to be this clumsy, I would have drawn up a breakage clause and demanded that you sign it."

Jeremy couldn't decide which incensed him more—her saying he was clumsy, or her none-too-subtle reference to the clever way she'd managed to snarl him up in a complex legal tangle. "And if I'd known you'd turn out to be such a niggardly nitpicker, I would have left you at the altar."

Refusing to embroil herself in another heated slanging match when the atmosphere inside the kitchen was already well within the danger zone, Maddy made an attempt to ease the acute tension. "Hindsight is always twenty-twenty," she agreed in a soothing tone. "Hopefully things will look much better to both of us in the morning."

Jeremy glared at her as he dropped a handful of broken porcelain into the garbage pail under the sink. "Thank you for those comforting platitudes," he spat out contemptuously. "Now I can add *patronizing* and *trite* to my growing list of your questionable talents."

Maddy's generosity only extended so far, and with those insulting remarks, Jeremy had stepped well over the line. "And I can add *stupid* and *childish* to the list I'm compiling on you."

"'Stupid'!" Jeremy exclaimed, then decided that he disliked her second label even more. "'Childish'!"

With a smug lift to her chin, Maddy jerked the stopper out of the drain, then turned on her heel and, head held high, started away from the sink. "Unlike you, *Master* Kincaid," she observed loftily, "I've matured well beyond the point of temper tantrums."

The woman had pushed him too far, and before he considered the possible ramifications of his reckless action, Jeremy had grabbed hold of her arm and swung her back around to face him. "Is that so, Miss Priss?" he challenged angrily, thrusting up her chin with one hand and using his other arm to anchor her in place. "Let's just see how mature a woman you really are."

At first Maddy fought him, pummeling his chest with her clenched fists. But then he had her mouth trapped under his, her body backed up against the kitchen counter, and she completely forgot what she was fighting for. It was the wildest, deepest, most shocking kiss Maddy had ever received from a man, and she was so stunned by the matching hunger it inspired in her that all she could do was helplessly respond—breathlessly, eagerly respond. After a few moments of indulgence in a pleasure so ruthless that it overwhelmed all her senses, Jeremy pressed his advantage and gentled the kiss, easing the abrasive feel of his beard against her smooth cheeks and savoring her soft, moist lips as if they were a rare and precious delicacy that he'd waited his entire lifetime to taste.

Tasting him back, Maddy felt a delightful warmth radiating outward from some deep, inner core, and she melted more fully against him, her trembling lower body seeking the strong cradle of his muscular thighs. She felt his shocking receptiveness to her surrender, and the pleasurable heat intensified, flaming higher and higher with every restless movement of her hips. Jeremy inhaled sharply at the provocative contact and he tightened his fingers on her face in a last, useless attempt to maintain his control. Punishing her no longer mattered, but possessing her did, and his more primal instincts took over.

As he thrust inside her mouth with his tongue, temporarily satisfying one hunger, he brought both arms behind her back, even more desperate to assuage another. Cupping her beautifully rounded buttocks in his hands, he lifted her up, unable to prevent his groan of pleasure as he fitted her softness against his hardened flesh. He didn't know which action was to blame for the sudden stiffening in her body or the sharp jab he felt in his ribs, but a second later, Jeremy was left holding nothing but a fleeting ache in his middle. Before he could draw a decent breath, too dazed to comprehend exactly what had happened, Maddy was out of the room and well on her way up the stairs.

It was a golden morning with the sun flaming up over the mountains and dancing through the cracks in the closed shutters, jolting Maddy awake. The invigorating chill that filled the air had her scrambling out of bed, anxious to be outside, even if her brain still felt fuzzy from lack of sleep. Hopping from one bare foot to another on the cold floor of the loft, she rummaged through her suitcases until she located what she wanted, then swiftly pulled off her flannel nightgown.

Shivering, she drew on a pair of lined jeans, a longsleeved red flannel shirt, a thick pair of woolen socks and her cowhide boots. Then, praying that Jeremy was still asleep, she picked up the bag containing her toothbrush and crept silently down the stairs. Considering what had happened between them after supper last night, she could go days and days without the pleasure of seeing him again. And seeing him again would indeed be a pleasure, she acknowledged with a rueful grimace.

For some reason, that...that *stockbroker* had a devastating effect on her libido, and no matter what she did, Maddy didn't seem to have any control over it. She knew he was a fraud, a conniving wolf in shepherd's clothing, but damnation, if he didn't look absolutely terrific in the disguise. Too bad that looks weren't everything, Maddy thought, scowling as she contemplated her susceptibility to a pair of bedroom eyes.

All Jeremy had to do was glance at her with those dark, molten orbs of his and she felt as if she were burning up from the inside out. Knowing who he really was and where he came from, she felt her sexual reaction to him was totally ridiculous. It was crazy and awful; but over and beyond that, it was downright confusing.

After two broken engagements, she'd taken a pledge never to give her heart again, but when it came to Jeremy, her body didn't seem willing to go along with the program. In his letters, Jeremy had seemed like such a nice guy, a man who might not excite her sexually, but whom she could always count on as a friend. Like a fool, she'd convinced herself that he needed her as much as she needed him. Unlike the past men in her life, she'd considered him to be safe.

"Hah!" Maddy scoffed, as she pushed open the door off the hall and made her way to the outhouse. "Double hah!"

Fifteen minutes later, she stood on the front steps of the lodge and took a deep, cleansing breath of fresh air. Deliberately she banished any and all unsettling thoughts about Jeremy from her mind. For a short while this morning, she had only herself for company, and she intended to enjoy her time alone. With that resolution firmly in mind, she started down the trail toward the lake, her smile growing wider with each step.

As a young girl growing up on the farm, mornings had always been her favorite time of day. A lovely serenity marked these early hours, a peaceful recess period that Mother Nature kindly provided for the exclusive use of birds and the small furry creatures that scampered like playful children through the dew-drenched undergrowth of the forest. All around her, Maddy could sense motion, even if she couldn't see what was rustling beneath the lacy fronds of wild fern or stirring the delicate pink and white flowers that bloomed beside the pine-strewn path.

Even the puffy white clouds seemed at play, Maddy thought as she glanced upward to watch them scudding back and forth in the salmon-colored sky. A second later, however, she heard a loud, crashing noise to her right, and turned her head in time to see a huge cow moose, no more than ten feet away from her, rushing toward the lake, a newborn calf at her heels. Stunned by the close encounter, Maddy leaned back against a tree to recover her breath, but as she watched the baby moose splashing through the shallows, gamboling beneath the fine spray of white water set off by its mother's stamping hooves, she stopped being afraid. Somehow she sensed that the huge moose was no more a threat to her than she was to it. Just like her, mother and child were delighting in the start of a fresh new day, and in this brief golden span of time, there could be no danger, no enemies.

As Maddy broke through the trees onto the rocky beach, she heard a series of shrill cries and looked up to see a half-dozen graceful white birds circling the water. Like an aerial acrobatic group, they seemed to dance with the air, gliding downward to touch the water lightly with their beaks, then sweeping upward again to soar through the sky. To Maddy, it seemed as if they were calling out to each other in sheer joy, rejoicing in their effortless motions through space.

"Those are arctic terns. They've just come back from the other end of the world in order to find mates and raise their young. In another week or so, there'll be hundreds of them."

At the unexpected and highly unwelcome sound of that gravelly voice, Maddy whirled about and found Jeremy, coffee mug in hand, perched upon a nearby boulder. He was dressed much as she was, in jeans and a flannel shirt, though his feet were bare. Judging by the soap and towel lying on the ground next to him, he'd just taken a bath in the lake. His sable-brown hair was still gleaming wet, the droplets of moisture glistened like tiny diamonds in his full beard. Since Maddy hadn't expected to have to share the morning, the fact that he was taking equal pleasure in the view thoroughly annoyed her.

"Are you always up and about this early?" she demanded churlishly.

He raised one dark brow in surprise at her tone, but then he grinned. "A bit of a grump in the morning, are we?"

Maddy felt her cheeks grow warm beneath his probing gaze, and she wished she'd taken the time to run a quick comb through her hair. Normally she woke up all bright-eyed and bushy tailed, but she'd tossed and turned for most of the night, and fixing her hair and applying makeup had seemed like too much of an effort. She disliked being caught with a face devoid of all color, and a bunch of unruly curls sticking out all over her head; but then she noticed that Jeremy wasn't staring at her hair.

Forcing herself not to lift her hand to the telltale whisker burn on her right cheek, she replied truthfully, "Not usually. I just didn't get much sleep last night."

"Me, either," Jeremy admitted, frowning slightly as he glanced away from her and pointed to a thermos bottle he'd placed on a flat rock next to him. "If you want hot coffee, you can use the top of that for a cup."

Maddy hesitated, resenting his disruption of her solitude, but then she resigned herself to his unwelcome presence and accepted his offer. "Thanks," she mumbled, as she took a tentative sip and discovered that the hot brew was made just the way she liked it— not too strong and not too bitter.

"Pull up a rock," Jeremy suggested, patting a flat outcropping of stone next to him. "If you want to watch the early show, these are the two best seats in the house."

Warily, Maddy considered his suggestion. She wasn't ready for another verbal sparring match with him this early in the morning, but she thought she'd detected a note of challenge in his voice, and she wasn't about to back down from it. She'd done quite enough of that yesterday, she decided, and recalling how she'd escaped to her room last night—unable to face him after the way she'd responded to his kisses— verbal contests weren't the only thing she was going to have to contend with.

Of course, she had only herself to blame for that humiliating little skirmish in the kitchen, Maddy reminded herself. She'd goaded him too far. But that knowledge didn't provide much comfort. Even though she'd somehow managed to struggle out of his embrace before the situation had gotten totally out of hand, she hadn't done so before she'd revealed just how much she liked the taste of him. Now that they were both aware of that, it wouldn't take much to touch off another sexual confrontation; and considering what a bad showing she'd made of herself the last time, Maddy wasn't ready for another one of those.

To her surprise, Jeremy didn't say anything else to her or make any sudden, dangerous moves as she sat down beside him, but kept his attention focused on the moose and her calf who were still wading in the shallows. After a few moments of acute tension, Maddy relaxed her vigilance and enjoyed the rest of her coffee.

"I like mornings best," Jeremy said, once he was sure that she wasn't going to bolt. After the way he'd forced himself on her last night, he wouldn't have blamed her if she didn't want to come anywhere near him. Then again, she hadn't exactly pushed him away when he'd kissed her—at least, not until he'd brought his tongue into play. He would have been satisfied with just one kiss if Maddy hadn't pressed her hips against him and moaned as if she were dying for it. How was he supposed to resist a temptation like that?

Jeremy clenched his coffee cup as he considered the fact that he'd never had any trouble resisting a woman before. No matter how seductively she behaved or how beautiful she was, he'd maintained his perspective. But Maddy got to him without even half trying; and that terrified him. At an early age, he'd learned what happens to a man who allowed a woman too much power over his emotions, and he'd sworn that no female would ever get that close to him. But Maddy cut through his defenses as if they weren't there.

If he were honest with himself, he would have to admit that his uncharacteristic behavior around her was a direct result of that deep-seated fear. As wrong as she was for him, Maddy also had the capability of warming a dark, cold place in his soul, a place that before she'd entered his life, had always resisted touching. Understanding that, the instant she'd admitted that she'd lied to him about her background and qualifications, he should have turned the plane around and dumped her back at Big Sal's. Unfortunately he hadn't done that. And now he knew that if he didn't get rid of her as quickly as possible, he was in very big trouble.

"Me, too."

Jeremy jerked his head around to look at her. *"What?"*

Maddy's expression turned quizzical as she pondered the startled look on his face. "I like mornings best, too."

"Oh," Jeremy said, and smiled at her—the first truly friendly smile he'd given her since he'd found out that she wasn't just a simple farm girl.

In the surprisingly peaceful silence that followed, both Maddy and Jeremy settled back and gazed across the mirrorlike surface of the lake, until Maddy noticed a ring forming on the water. Shortly thereafter, another appeared perhaps twenty feet away from the first, and then another and another, without any visible cause.

Before she could ask, Jeremy told her. "Lake trout. They've started coming up from deep water to feed on the larvae and baby herring near the shore. See that?"

Maddy looked to where he was pointing and saw a streak of silver and another widening ring in the water. "Wow! That fish looked plenty big."

Jeremy nodded. "I'd say about a fifteen-pounder, which makes him as old as you are."

"Really?"

Jeremy grinned at her surprise. "Just like the growth of far northern timber, fish mature more slowly up here. Those that make it to over twenty pounds have lived longer than *I* have."

As she'd been several times yesterday, Maddy was impressed by the depth of his knowledge. "For a city slicker, you sure seem to know a lot about the wildlife around here. Did Joe give you a crash course? Or did you get all of these fascinating facts out of books?"

Maddy hadn't meant to sound sarcastic, but she didn't like the feeling that Jeremy knew so much more about life in the wilds than she did. After all, *she* was the one who'd grown up close to nature, not him. Her rough-and-ready mountain man had been raised in the asphalt jungle. During supper last night, he'd admitted that of all places, he'd been born and raised in Brooklyn.

Unfortunately, Maddy couldn't unsay the envious question, and it only took one look at him for her to understand that she'd lost any ground she might have previously gained. "You're really determined not to like me, aren't you?" Jeremy asked, and he didn't sound the least bit disappointed at the possibility.

After that shocking but marvelously satisfying kiss they'd shared, Maddy couldn't help but be a little hurt by his uncaring attitude, and her reply was sharp. "I believe that the intent is mutual."

"Maybe," he allowed, then reversed the claim she'd made about herself the night before. "But at least I'm mature enough to restrain my animosity toward you until we figure out what we're going to do about this mess."

His expression told her exactly what he would like to do, but Maddy had no intention of jumping off the nearest cliff. "I don't know what you're going to do," she replied coldly. "But I'm going to help get this lodge ready for our first guests, just like I told you I would."

"You also told me you knew one end of a hammer from another," he reminded her scornfully. "Which I now have good reason to doubt."

Maddy knew she'd exaggerated somewhat in her letters, but she wasn't the only one who'd stretched the truth to suit her own purposes. "And I have equally good reason to doubt that you know any more about that than I do."

"I spent an entire summer working construction, and I'll have you know that I was very good at my job."

Unimpressed, Maddy shot back, "Well, I helped my grandfather build a barn, and my brother and I built our playhouse from the ground up. People from miles around came to admire it."

"Playhouse?" Jeremy pounced on that admission like a hungry cat after a defenseless mouse. "Exactly how old were you at the time?"

"Old enough to get the job done," Maddy mumbled defensively.

"I'll just bet," Jeremy gritted through his teeth, then growled, "Why can't you see that this is never going to work? You don't belong in a place like this, and you damned well know it. A woman like you isn't fit for this kind of life."

"As far as I can tell, I'm as fit as you are."

Without another word, Jeremy stood up from his seat. "Since it's obvious that you're one of the most muleheaded females I've ever run across in my life, this discussion could drag on all day. We might as well continue it up in the lodge where we'll be more comfortable."

"That's fine with me," Maddy agreed, stalling for time by replacing the top on the thermos and picking up Jeremy's cup and towel.

Unfortunately, Jeremy didn't stalk off and leave her to follow as she expected him to do, but waited for her to precede him up the trail. When she didn't immediately comply with his unspoken request, he grabbed her by the wrist and forcibly assisted her along.

"Let go of me, you Neanderthal!" Maddy protested when she couldn't break free of his hold.

"'Neanderthal,' am I?" Jeremy asked with a mocking grin as he pulled her behind him. "And only yesterday you were calling me a namby-pamby desk jockey."

"Yesterday you weren't manhandling me like this! I detest being manhandled!"

Jeremy stopped so fast that Maddy ran into him, and she couldn't react fast enough when he wrapped his hand around her throat and jerked up her chin. "No, you don't," he growled, his dark eyes blazing down on her flushed face. "Last night you showed me just how much you like a little of the rough stuff, and you've still got the marks on your skin left to prove it."

Suddenly Maddy became aware that Jeremy seemed more angry with himself than with her. Though his eyes burned into her face like hot coals, the stroke of his thumb against the reddened patch of skin on her cheek was astonishingly gentle. It was also extremely tantalizing, and set off a series of exciting shivers in her body. To her dismay, Maddy saw that he was well aware of her reaction to his touch.

"Namby-pamby or Neanderthal, I still did this to your face," he reminded her gruffly, a muscle twitching in his cheek as he ran one finger over her bottom lip and felt her responsive tremble. "And you liked it."

"I didn't want to like it," Maddy whispered helplessly, swaying toward him as if hypnotized.

"But you did. So unless you pack up and leave while you still can," he warned fiercely, "I'm going to mark you again."

Dropping his hands to her shoulders to hold those soft, delectable breasts of hers away from his chest, he rasped, "And next time, it's going to be a lot worse."

"It...it doesn't have to happen that way, not if...if we stick to our original agreement to be friends first and lovers later," Maddy stammered idiotically, unable to stop herself from staring at his mouth. She could almost feel those lips dividing hers, feel his caressing tongue.

Jeremy felt an uncomfortable tightening in his loins. The damnable woman was doing it to him again, tempting him almost beyond endurance; but this time he was certain she was deliberately seducing him. And unlike last night, he wasn't going to break under the sensual pressure of those moist, parted lips and compelling blue eyes. "If we can't abide by those terms, then will you give up and leave?"

Maddy shook her head, as her gaze shifted higher. He really had the most incredibly gorgeous eyes, offset by the longest, gold-tipped lashes she'd ever seen on a man. And when he was angry those beautiful eyes sparkled like flames—deep, dark, beckoning flames. "I...I know it won't be easy, but if we're willing to work at it, I think we could still make this marriage succeed."

Jeremy let out an oath. "My God, woman! You're really asking for it!"

"I'm not asking you for anything, but a little human kindness," Maddy exclaimed indignantly, shocked out of her sensual trance.

"'Kindness'!" Jeremy scoffed. "You were asking me for a hell of a lot more than that just now, and you know it!"

"Okay, so I find you attractive," Maddy admitted, a bit desperately. "So what? That doesn't mean we have to hop right into bed together. I'm perfectly willing to wait until we've established a nice, workable relationship."

"How *kind* of you," Jeremy declared sarcastically. "But unfortunately, I haven't had a woman in months, so if you insist on being my wife, I'm going to make you one in every sense of the word."

"Then you *did* lie to me in all those letters," Maddy accused, her expression scornful.

"Don't make me say this again, lady, or you'll be very sorry. I am not, I repeat, *not* a liar!"

"Well, the man I thought I married made me several promises in writing, and waiting to have sex until we were both ready was one of them."

"You seemed ready enough a few minutes ago," Jeremy pointed out, the gravelly edge to his voice more pronounced than ever.

"Well, I'm not now," Maddy retorted. "And if you don't stop pressuring me, I don't know if I ever will be."

Jeremy ran a frustrated hand through his hair as he glared down at her. "Let me see if I've got this straight," he bit out acidly, fighting for control of his temper. "You intend for us to stay married, but we can't have sex until you decide the time is right. Of course, you can bat those baby blues at me and rub up against me all you want with that sexy body of yours, but I'm not supposed to do anything about it because I promised to give you all the time you need. Is that about right?"

This time Maddy realized that his anger was directed exclusively at her, and she was also aware that she deserved it. She *had* been staring at him as if she could eat him up. Even though she hadn't been conscious at the time of what she was doing, it had to have appeared to him as if she were deliberately leading him on. The only excuse she had for her provocative behavior was that his sexy self had provoked it. But she didn't think he would appreciate that explanation. Nor would he buy the excuse that she hadn't been aware of what she was doing.

Supposedly she was a sophisticated woman of the world, who, when it came to worldly-wise men, knew the score. But she didn't. God help her. She should have, but still she didn't. And there lay the crux of her problem.

She'd been engaged twice, and she still didn't know diddly squat about the fine old art of female seduction. If she *had* known more about wielding her body to her best advantage, she might have had a better understanding of how to handle the treacherous male of the species. As it was, all she'd learned from her past relationships was that experienced men didn't appreciate heartfelt emotion in a woman unless they needed it to bolster their own egos.

It was her opinion that most males wanted sex, and when a woman didn't give it to them as often as they wanted it, they went looking for someone who would. Grant Parsons, the photographer who'd first discovered her and then put an engagement ring on her finger to ensure his place in her budding career, hadn't suffered a moment's guilty feeling over his unfaithfulness to her. He'd viewed her fresh-faced beauty as something he could sell and her young body as something he could use until a newer face and lovelier body came to town.

Both he and Paul Hastings, the account executive who'd chosen her to launch the Dew Drop campaign, had known how much she loved them, but neither of them had been capable of returning that feeling in a way that met her expectations. At least possessing her body had been enough for Grant. But in his role as her mentor, Paul had wanted to control every aspect of her life, including her thoughts.

With Jeremy, love wasn't an issue, but it looked like the sex thing still was. Just like Grant, he wanted her body. He didn't even like her—certainly didn't respect her—and yet he still desired her. That angered her more than anything else. She wasn't just a body; she was a thinking, feeling person who deserved better treatment.

"I wouldn't have outlined the terms of our association so crudely," she finally replied in an icy tone. "But then, I'm a woman, and unlike you, all my actions aren't governed by my hormones. I'm sorry if you assumed I was issuing you a sexual invitation. I wasn't. I was only admiring your looks. I just keep forgetting that men consider a friendly smile a come-on, and think that one harmless kiss entitles them to a free passion session."

His nostrils flaring at her condescending tone, Jeremy spat out, "If you considered that kiss 'harmless,' lady, I can't wait to see what kind of damage you'll do the next time we try it. And as your husband, let me remind you that I'm legally entitled to an endless amount of those 'free sessions.'"

More than a little intimidated by that threat, Maddy couldn't hide the note of panic in her voice, nor the shimmer of tears in her eyes. "And I thought I'd finally found a man who was different from the rest—a man who had a little sensitivity. But I should have known better. No matter what they promise you, men only want one thing from a woman, and they'll lie and cheat, do any rotten thing they have to, in order to get it!"

"Maddy, I—" Jeremy drew back his hand before his fingers could touch her, shocked by the depth of hurt and disillusionment he saw in her eyes. Her judgment of him was so unfair, and the stubborn stance she'd taken about their marriage so unrealistic that he'd retaliated in anger. But he'd never expected to provoke this kind of reaction. Though he was aware she'd been hurt by other men, he'd had no way of knowing that her wounds went so deep, or that they were still open and bleeding. "Maddy, I never wanted—"

"You never wanted what?" she interrupted him bitterly. "Never wanted me as a friend? Never wanted me as your business partner? You don't have to tell me what you never wanted, Jeremy. I've already figured it out."

Stung by her outburst, he declared. "If you really believe that about me, then you should have also reached the conclusion that our marriage doesn't stand a chance."

"I'd say it stands just as good a chance as any," Maddy retorted cynically. "I want a home and children, and you want a convenient bed partner. Isn't that the basis for all marriages?"

"I want more than that, Maddy, and so do you," Jeremy surprised himself by saying. "We both deserve more than that."

Maddy's tone was flat. "Maybe, but that's all I'm expecting to get out of it. Maybe that's all any woman gets."

Jeremy gritted his teeth to keep from shouting. "What about what I want and expect, Maddy? Don't my feelings count for anything?"

Maddy lifted her chin, but Jeremy saw more pride than defiance in her expression.

"I'm sorry I'm not the woman you expected, Jeremy, but I've burnt all of my bridges behind me. For me, there's no going back."

"So unless I sue you for a divorce, we're stuck with each other."

She lifted her chin another notch. "I guess so."

Jeremy stared into her eyes for a long moment, then walked away before he became violent.

"Is that what you plan to do?" Maddy called after him as he stalked swiftly up the trail. "Divorce me?"

"I'll let you know," he called back.

Maddy ran to catch up with him. "If you do that, I'll still be your business partner, and that means I've got the legal right to stay here as long as I want to. And I don't intend to be a silent partner, Kincaid. From here on in, I intend to be involved in every decision that's made."

Jeremy kept on walking, but the instant she came abreast of him, he warned, "Give it a rest, Maddy."

"Not until you tell me what you intend to do," she persisted, then made the mistake of grabbing his arm.

For a second he looked as if he wanted to strike her, but then a shutter came down over his face, and a peculiar expression entered his eyes.

"You've got guts, Maddy," he informed her gruffly. "I'll say that much for you. And that's only one of the things that never came across in your letters. It makes me wonder what else I don't know about you."

"Probably the same amount as I don't know about you."

"On the other hand, there are a lot of things we *do* know, aren't there?" he inquired, as a strange new note entered his voice. "For instance, when the time comes, we both know that we're going to be dynamite in bed."

Abruptly aware of the heat emanating from his skin, Maddy snatched her hand away from his arm. "*If* the time comes," she amended. "Which it won't if you decide to divorce me."

Jeremy's expression was dangerous. "That sounds a lot like blackmail. Do you always barter your body in order to get what you want from a man?"

"I'd never do that!" Maddy cried, horrified by that erroneous assumption.

"That's good," Jeremy told her, with a predatory smile. "Because the bedroom is one area where I could beat you at your own game."

Maddy gulped at his claim, for there was no doubt in her mind that it was true. Just watching him breathe was a pleasure, and if he ever flexed all that virile muscle in her direction, she would probably suffer a complete meltdown. Flushing at the possibility of that happening, Maddy stammered, "In...in your letters, you...you didn't strike me as the type of man who enjoyed playing childish, sexual games."

Slowly, deliberately, Jeremy brought up his hand beneath her chin, stroking her soft cheek as he gazed deeply into her eyes. To Maddy it seemed as if he were searching for something inside her, and then his eyes flickered as if he'd found it.

"I'm not," he agreed. "But adult games are a different story, and when I decide to enter one of those, I play for keeps."

As Jeremy leaned forward, Maddy closed her eyes, with a mixture of fear and anticipation on her face. She was certain he was going to kiss her again, and she wanted him to—almost as badly as she wanted him to back off. Then, just as the wanting part of her won out over the frightened part, Jeremy dropped his hand away from her face and swiftly stepped back.

"You know?" he asked softly as her eyes flew open in shock. "It could be that you're not such a ditsy blonde, after all. Maybe you're just a woman who's been hurt so badly that she doesn't know what she wants anymore, and is too afraid to risk finding out."

Embarrassed by his perception, Maddy asserted rashly, "Don't assume I'm afraid of you, Jeremy Kincaid. Because that assumption would be wrong."

Instead of responding to the desperate challenge in her tone, Jeremy took another step away from her, frustration etched into his features. "Then you have the advantage over me, lady, because I'm scared to death of you."

"You are?" Maddy murmured incredulously.

"I am, but I'll be damned before I give you the satisfaction of calling me a coward to my face. And I can be just as stubborn as you, therefore I'm going to stick this thing out just as long as you do."

"You are?"

"I am," Jeremy told her, then realized that he'd just stepped into the trap he'd vowed to avoid. "But for both our sakes," he continued, backpedaling as much as he could without actually turning tail and running, "I don't think we should make this a lifetime sentence. What would you say to a trial period?"

"'A trial period'?"

She seemed willing to consider that concession, so Jeremy immediately pressed for verbal compliance. "Say five or six months? Then, if we're still not getting along, we won't be trapped together over the winter."

Still befuddled by his announcement that he was frightened of her, Maddy had trouble getting her tongue to function properly. "Th-that sounds fair."

"Then it's a deal?" Jeremy asked, pulling one hand from his pocket and sticking it out toward her.

Maddy shook it before he could change his mind. "Deal."

Five

_____

After two weeks of cooperative, oftentimes frustrating effort, Maddy and Jeremy had finally reached the final installment in the book *Home Plumbing Made Easy*. Wisely, Maddy had forced herself not to comment when Jeremy made a mistake; and in return, Jeremy had kept his mouth shut when *she*'d done something wrong. All in all, the frequent manifestation of their ineptitudes had been a humbling experience for them both.

On the other hand, they were each too stubborn to give up and admit that they weren't up to the challenge. So all that was left for them to do today was open up the hot- and cold-water valves and pray that there was a safe amount of pressure in their new pipes. At least they had the security of knowing that Randy Owens and his plumbing crew from Fairbanks had done the more difficult, underground hookup work from the outside well to the lodge. Randy's men had also installed the hot-water heater and the interior pipes to the kitchen and bath, but that still didn't mean that the shower stall would hold water or the toilet flush without leaking.

"I wish we'd let Randy handle the whole job," Maddy conceded, worrying her lower lip with her teeth as she watched Jeremy contort his large body into a yoga position in order to reach the knobs behind the white porcelain toilet. "What if we've done something wrong? We could have a flood in here and ruin all our good work."

"At two hundred dollars an hour, we couldn't afford Randy for another day, let alone a week," Jeremy reminded her as he straightened up without cracking his head on the newly installed fixture. "Besides, compared to what they had to do, this part of the job was a piece of cake."

"Let's just pray the cake doesn't fall," Maddy retorted, holding her breath as Jeremy lifted the top off the toilet tank and peered inside.

"Hey! It's filling up," he announced triumphantly, as if he were witnessing some kind of miracle.

Considering her own Herculean efforts in trying to convert this cramped storage closet into a usable bathroom, Maddy couldn't help but feel a similar pride in their accomplishments. Their success might not seem like much to most people, but she felt like the cat who'd just eaten the canary, and she could tell that Jeremy felt the same way. After all, here they were, two city people who didn't know the first thing about plumbing, and yet, with a little common sense and the help of an instructive how-to book, they'd managed to install an entire bathroom themselves.

"Will you just look at that!" she declared, clapping her hands together in glee as the water reached the top of the tank and the plunger automatically fell down to shut off the trap. "So far so good. But in the face of a possible deluge, do we dare flush?"

"As commander of my own fate, I'll bravely accept that challenge," Jeremy declared, his grin as wide as Maddy's as he pushed down on the stainless-steel handle. "There she blows!"

Maddy felt the unvarnished, wooden slats vibrate beneath her bare feet and heard an ominous rumble inside the freshly painted walls, but other than that, the flushing process was completed with no visible problems. "Victory!" she shouted in exultation, smirking as she noticed how quickly Jeremy had managed to roll up the pant legs of his jeans.

"Just in case," he admitted sheepishly.

"Does this mean you're now ready to march on to the shower stall, commander?"

With a flourishing bow, Jeremy proclaimed, "Madam, in view of your dedicated application of paint, elbow grease and putty, I hereby bestow that honor upon you."

Maddy gave him a pert curtsy, but the movement brought her elbow into painful contact with the new sink. "Thank you—I think," she replied dryly, ever mindful of splinters as she cautiously moved her foot sideways in the tight quarters. "Have you noticed that two people don't fit very well in here? We can barely breathe without getting personal."

Being pals with her for fourteen of the longest days in his life, Jeremy knew there weren't any underlying sexual connotations to that comment, which was exactly the reason he was tempted to make a less-than-innocent response. He was fast losing patience with their platonic relationship, especially since Maddy was looking better and better to him every day. Since he also realized that the only reason she'd lost that tense, pinched look around her mouth and the dark circles under her eyes was because she'd started to trust him, Jeremy found himself between a rock and a hard place.

Behaving like a friend instead of a lover had taxed his willpower to the maximum, but that wasn't the only difficulty he'd had to contend with. During the past two weeks, he'd also had to come to grips with the fact that he wanted a woman who was never going to be the docile wife he'd imagined for himself. Out to prove her equality, Maddy had matched him step for step, forcing him to reevaluate most of the male chauvinist roles he'd projected on the "fair" sex.

Although he'd never in his life come across a woman who always expected to pull her own weight even if she didn't quite know how to do it, he had to respect Maddy's willingness to try. It had also been brought home to him the fact that his survival skills weren't that much better than hers. As a man, he was physically strong; but with Maddy, that was the only advantage he had. As much as he hated to admit it, he couldn't help but marvel at the way she tackled every new problem that came her way with boundless enthusiasm.

Not only that, but thus far, she'd also done her share of the cooking, and more than her share of the cleaning. With nary a complaint, she'd worked side by side with him, and while engaged in their daily labors, she worked up a sweat—good, old-fashioned, honest sweat. To Jeremy's amazement, she hadn't complained about that, either.

This morning she not only smelled pretty, but as on every day since they'd started on this project, she was dressed in short denim cutoffs that outlined her delectable derriere, and a skimpy cotton top that clung lovingly to her breasts. Yesterday, as he'd lain on his back working under the sink, she'd been forced to step across his body exactly forty-two times. He'd counted every crossing, and viewing her provocative curves and long slender legs from that angle had caused him endless suffering. He didn't want to scare her off, yet controlling his intense physical response to her was all but driving him crazy.

With a pained sigh, Jeremy forced himself to stay on the neutral ground they'd established as he edged cautiously closer to where she was standing. "You have to admit that it's better than the outhouse."

"How true, how true," Maddy agreed, and reached inside the shower stall to turn on both spigots.

This time she felt no concern as she heard the harmless rumble in the pipes, but when she looked up and saw that no water was coming out of the shower head, her face fell. "Something's wrong," she observed worriedly, peering up through the open door and stretching out her arm to fiddle with the stainless-steel fixture. "Nothing's coming out."

"Here, let me see," Jeremy said, ducking under her arm to step inside the enclosure. But even after he'd turned the temperature regulator in both directions, from cold to hot and back again, nothing happened. Hands on his hips, he stared at the simple fixture, trying to figure out the problem. "Maybe this thing is defective."

"I doubt it." Maddy shook her head, unaware of Jeremy's sharp intake of breath as she joined him inside the stall. Wedging herself in front of him, she peered under the fixture and noticed a second, short handle. "Have you tried this? Aah!"

As a blast of cold water hit him in the face, Jeremy reeled backward, but there was no escape from the torrential downpour. "Shut it off!" he sputtered helplessly, then promptly lost his footing as Maddy twisted away from the spray and knocked him off balance. The thin aluminum sides of the enclosure were smooth, and with nothing to hang on to, Jeremy slid down the back wall, ending up in a half-prone position on the metal floor, seated amid a quickly rising pool of water.

"Dammit, Maddy, shut it off!" He demanded again, as the ice-cold spray soaked into his jeans. "Nothing's going down the drain!"

Arms flailing, Maddy tried to relocate the shut-off handle but, blinded by the frigid shower, she had a hard time finding it again. Then, just as she finally located it, Jeremy let out a pained yowl and clamped a wet hand around her bare leg. "Watch where you're stepping, woman!"

With a startled squeak, Maddy jumped away from his icy touch, but that proved to be her downfall. Her feet slipped out from under her, and she fell, her bottom landing with a squishy plop on Jeremy's lap. As she struggled frantically to get back up, her hands sliding uselessly along the wet walls, she heard a loud series of bangs, camouflaging the pained groans coming from the man trapped beneath her. "It sounds like the pipes are going to explode!"

"I know the feeling," Jeremy grunted as she squirmed around on his lap.

"Will you kindly get up?" Maddy pleaded in exasperation.

"Have a heart," Jeremy begged, as her soft bottom settled snugly between his spread legs. Such inhumane punishment demanded retribution, and Jeremy was no longer capable of resisting temptation. "Not that this isn't romantic, you understand. But wouldn't you rather attempt this kind of gymnastics in a warm, dry bed?"

"Oh, Lord," Maddy breathed in growing desperation as she scooted forward to find that the only way she could avoid the spray was to twist sideways and bury her face in his soggy midsection.

"I guess not," Jeremy surmised, the huge grin he wore earning him a well-deserved mouthful of cold water and a small fist in the stomach.

"You are *not* a nice person," Jeremy accused. Yet there was no malice in his tone. "Of course, under these exciting circumstances, who cares?"

"Jeremy!" Maddy felt his growing arousal against her thigh, and wanted to hit him, but with the ever-increasing pressure of the cold water spraying down on their torsos and heads, she gave up on her attempts to stand.

Muttering a most unladylike oath, she pushed down on Jeremy's bent knee and lifted herself over his leg. "Now you can get up!"

"Ah, you're no fun at all," Jeremy complained as she wiggled down into a seated position beside him, hugging her legs with her arms.

"You've got a very weird sense of humor, Kincaid." Maddy lowered her head to evade the brunt of the spray, but out of the corner of her eye, she saw the water slosh over the shallow rim of the stall. "For crying out loud, Jeremy, *do* something," she wailed. "Right now, you idiot, before we get water all over my brand-new wood floor."

"We've already done that," Jeremy informed her cheerfully, still smiling, though he no longer had any excuse to remain where he was.

"Ever think of trying this?" he inquired, as he struggled to his feet, turned off the taps, then reached up and switched the small, troublesome handle on the shower head into the off position. "This would've been a far more pleasant experience if the water had been warm."

"I doubt it," Maddy grumbled through chattering teeth.

"What the hell could be wrong with this drain?" Jeremy pondered out loud, looking down at his feet, which were covered by a good three inches of water. "It can't be clogged already."

"Maybe it's your brain that's clogged," Maddy suggested unkindly, swiping her dripping-wet hair off her face as she glared up at him.

But Jeremy wasn't paying any attention to her. Triumphantly, he proclaimed, "Here's the culprit!" and lifted a clear plastic lid from over the drain. "Problem solved."

"Wonderful," Maddy grumbled, wrapping her arms around her body to control her shivering.

Like a wet dog, Jeremy shook himself, and Maddy found herself on the receiving end of another shower as droplets of water flew out of his hair and beard.

"Stop that!" she ordered. "You're getting me all wet."

"Sorry," Jeremy apologized, his expression sincerely contrite.

It was then that Maddy was struck by the incongruity of her complaint and his apology. No matter what he did to her now, she could hardly get any wetter, and Jeremy was in no better shape. Water was still dripping off his beard; his blue work shirt and jeans were plastered to his skin, and he was shivering as violently as she was. "You look pathetic," she exclaimed, and started to giggle. "Just like a drowned rat."

Jeremy's lips twitched. "Well, what about you?" he asked, as he reached out a hand to help her stand up. "How does the description 'beached whale' strike you?"

"I'll have you know there's not an ounce of blubber on me," Maddy retorted indignantly, still laughing as she stepped after him out of the shower. A second later, her laughter died a swift death as Jeremy turned around, his eyes sweeping her body from head to toes as if trying to discover whether or not there was any truth to her boast.

Startled by his sudden interest in her body, Maddy stood as still as a statue, trying desperately to hide her interest in his body. Unfortunately Jeremy didn't make that very easy for her. Aware of her eyes on him, he stripped off his shirt, using his hands to whisk the water off his muscular arms. For two weeks she'd wondered what he would look like naked, and even though her curiosity wasn't going to be completely satisfied, she was greatly impressed with only a partial view.

Jeremy's chest was magnificent, his skin a burnished bronze. His shoulders were broad, his torso long and beautifully proportioned. His chest hair was dark and springy looking, and Maddy found herself watching in breathless fascination as a droplet of water trickled down the narrow strip leading to his navel. When the tiny rivulet was absorbed by the waistband of his jeans, Maddy felt an acute stab of disappointment.

Shocked by the intensity of her feelings, she wrenched her eyes upward toward his face to find him watching her—or at least, watching part of her. Jeremy's gaze wasn't on her face, but on another more provocative area of her body—her breasts—which to her dismay were now clearly visible through her wet, white cotton top.

"I can see that you're in great shape," Jeremy replied with a convulsive swallow.

"Jeremy," she warned. But he wasn't paying any attention.

He reached out for her, and she let him. Slowly, almost reluctantly, he tugged on her wrist, his hot gaze intent on her tight, rosy nipples that contracted even more beneath his visual caress. Then, when she was finally standing directly in front of him, he released her wrist and pronounced huskily. "You're exquisitely shaped—all over."

Maddy could feel the color of embarrassment staining her cheeks, but her benumbed brain refused all commands. She wanted to lift her hands to cover herself, but her arms hung limply at her sides, while an intense heat enveloped her body like a blanket. Jeremy wanted her. She could see that in the powerful muscles of his shoulders and neck that were tense and rigid, hear it in his harsh breathing. On the other hand, she could tell by the hesitant expression on his face that all she had to do to break the bonds of sensual tension that held them both immobile was to back away.

She couldn't bring herself to do that, however, and he gave her ample time, time enough to feel her breasts swell and her nipples throb with need; time enough to imagine the feel of his hands on her taut, aching flesh. She waited in an agony of anticipation, unable to look at him, yet unable to deny that she wanted him to touch her.

She drew in a deep, quivering breath, and then it came. His first light caress, like an electric shock that vibrated through her entire being.

Maddy closed her eyes, shamed by her lack of protest as he pushed the straps of her tank top off her shoulders and down her arms. A second later, her breasts were completely bared to his gaze. She felt cold, then hot as his hands swept upward over her rib cage, his warm palms brushing the excess moisture from her midriff as they swept ever higher.

By the time his hands reached the satiny curves of her breasts, Maddy's shivers could no longer be blamed on the cold. Every breath she drew seared through her as his palms cupped her, assessing her fullness, his thumbs testing the difference in texture between nipple and breast. For an instant, his exploration seemed almost clinical, but then he spoke in a voice so hoarse that Maddy could barely understand him.

"For weeks now, I've kept myself awake nights, thinking how the weight of you would feel in my hands." He lightly flicked her nipple with his thumbnail, and Maddy inhaled sharply. "How you'd harden and swell just for me. How I'd make you gasp with pleasure as you did just now. Do you ever think about what it would be like between us, Maddy? Have *you* lost any sleep thinking about it?"

Maddy shook her head in denial of the intense pleasure he was providing with his touch, but not in denial of her yearning. She was certain that she'd suffered through as many sleepless nights as he had, imagining them together just like this, thinking of her bare breasts enveloped by his large hands, his fingers stroking her skin. What she hadn't been able to foresee was the incredible depth of her response when dreams became reality.

"Have you?" Jeremy repeated in a gruff voice that rasped against her oversensitized nerves like the finest grade of sandpaper. When she still didn't answer, he compressed his hands and gently squeezed, then bent down and kissed one pert nipple. "Do you want me to stop?"

Maddy's eyes flew open to find him watching her, his expression so intense that it shocked her. To find her lost voice, however, she had to fight her way through a morass of sensuality that seemed to grow in power with every passing moment. "No," she managed to whisper as he lowered his head toward her again. "Oh, no... Don't stop... please."

Jeremy drew her nipple into his mouth, knowing that he was taking unfair advantage of her, but no longer caring. For once, her heart was controlling her head, and he was selfish enough to press his advantage while she was still in the throes of a momentary lapse of rationality. He'd been a very good boy up until now; perhaps *too* good, for Maddy's desire for him was obvious, as obvious as his desire for her. In that instant before he'd brought her fully into his mouth, he'd seen that her blue eyes were dark with passion, her cheeks flushed with it, and her breath uneven.

He felt her fingers tangling in his hair as he tasted her, felt her body sway as if her knees were growing weak, and he immediately brought his arms around to her back to prevent her from falling. Even then, with his hands cupping her buttocks, lifting her up and against him, she didn't panic. If he wanted to, he could take possession of her right then and she wouldn't do a thing to stop him. Unfortunately his conscience wouldn't let him go that far, even if she allowed it; but he needed to prove something to her, just as he needed to prove something to himself.

In Maddy, he'd finally met his match, his own personal Waterloo. Along with several other things, the last two weeks had taught him that. But he wanted her to start acknowledging the fact that she, too, was fighting a losing battle. She might not think she needed a man like him, but she was woman enough to need this, and at least that gave them a place to start. She'd made it clear that she wanted total equality in their relationship, and he intended to show her that when it came to a test of passion, their contest would end in a dead heat.

Maddy couldn't stand it. She couldn't breathe, could barely think. The feel of his lips on her breast, his stroking tongue, his hands moving up her bare back...and then much lower down, straying too close to the source of her ever-increasing torment. There were too many fiery sensations to absorb all at once, and she didn't like the feeling that she was starting to burn out of control, but she couldn't seem to quench the flames. Her body kept pressing closer to the fire, straining for something that Jeremy continued to withhold, and in the searing haze that enveloped, it felt as if he were taunting her on purpose.

Then, as his lips moved to her other breast, with his mustache and beard tingling along her soft flesh, Maddy became aware that she wasn't alone in her feelings: Jeremy was as aroused as she was. And with an abrupt motion he jerked his mouth away from her breast and pulled her half-naked body against his so she could feel the pounding of his heart and the heat of his skin. He was burning, just as she was, and his eyes in his flushed face were wild.

The moisture that remained on their skin was heated by their desire to form a liquid warmth that only added to their pleasure. Maddy bit her lower lip to suppress a moan as she rubbed herself against his chest, molding her body to his and straining for an even greater closeness. She did cry out when he drew back, but then his mouth was upon her once again, his teeth gently grazing the tip of her breast, nipping tenderly at the tightly puckered skin that had already been rendered unbearably sensitive.

An instant later, when Jeremy swore under his breath and grasped her by the shoulders to hold her away from him, Maddy didn't know where he found the strength, for his legs were just as unsteady as hers and his breath was coming in short, harsh gasps. Nor did she understand the regret in his eyes as he brought their lovemaking to a sudden halt, until he sharply decreed, "I never should have started this."

Stunned by his rejection, Maddy tried to pull away from him, but he held her fast. "I'm not saying I didn't like it,'' he said as if to explain, but his expression stated otherwise and Maddy renewed her struggle to escape.

''Maddy, I'm trying to say I'm sorry for hurting you. Look what I've done,'' he rasped, staring down at the reddened marks his ardor had left on her milky white skin. ''This beard has got to go, and the sooner the better! The next time I kiss you, I'm not going to do any physical damage.''

Putting action into words, he stalked out of the bathroom. ''I'll be back as soon as I get my razor.''

Maddy stared after him, first in astonishment, then in mounting panic as she realized that there had just occurred a dramatic change in their relationship. A second later, she gave in to the urge to flee. Like the sniveling, lily-livered weakling she was, she darted out of the room, and out the back door before she was forced to confront a reality she wasn't yet ready to accept.

Six

———

Jeremy sat down across from Maddy at the supper table, but to his annoyance she didn't acknowledge his presence by so much as a blink. "Don't you even have the guts to look at me?" he asked tersely as he cracked open a sourdough biscuit and helped himself to a generous portion of venison stew. "Maybe you'll like what you see."

"That's why I'm not looking," Maddy mumbled back, shoveling her food down as fast as she could without choking. "I'm no fool." But she was, Maddy knew, an utterly hopeless fool who was intensely drawn to a man that she knew was totally wrong for her; a man who had tricked her into believing that he was someone he was not.

Jeremy's spirits perked up considerably as he contemplated Maddy's response and he sat up straighter in his chair, smiling for the first time in hours. "And here I thought that after what happened between us this morning, you couldn't stand the sight of my face."

"Don't think, Kincaid," Maddy warned. "Thinking only makes a person realize what kind of trouble they're in."

"Am I giving you trouble?" Jeremy asked innocently. "What kind of trouble?"

"You know very well what kind!"

Jeremy grinned in satisfaction, reminded of a rhyme he'd heard in childhood. "Trouble is what you make it, and it isn't your distress that counts, but only how you take it. According to the way you responded to my kisses, Maddy, you take my brand of trouble very well."

"Cute, Kincaid," Maddy grumbled. "Very cute."

Lips twitching, Jeremy watched her spoon more stew into her mouth, then swallow a huge gulp of milk to assist it down her throat. "You can't avoid me forever, you know," he pointed out logically, no longer the least bit angry with her for deserting him in the bathroom, then disappearing for the rest of the day. Now he knew what she'd been running away from, and she had his total sympathy. "Eventually, you'll have to look at me again."

"Grow your beard back and I might think about it," Maddy suggested balefully.

Eyes dancing, Jeremy lifted his hand to his cleanly shaven jaw. "No way," he said. "You keep insisting that our relationship has to be fair and square, and this makes us even."

Maddy still didn't raise her head, but her furrowed brow told him that he'd pricked her curiosity. "How do you figure that?"

"Well," Jeremy began. "I've been forced to look at the face of the eighties for the last two weeks without swallowing my tongue, and it's only fair that you be subjected to the same kind of torture."

As Jeremy expected, that outrageous comment did the trick. "Of all the vain, egotistical... Oh, Lord..." Maddy's voice trailed off as she was confronted with Jeremy's unadorned features for the first time. *Tortured* was a good word to describe her feelings, for he was as rakishly handsome as she'd feared.

"Well?" he asked expectantly.

"Okay, so you weren't bragging," she allowed weakly, unable to stop herself from staring.

"If you say so," Jeremy replied with a devilish grin, showing off a set of dimples as perfect as her own.

"But it's still very impolite to toot one's own horn," she reminded him tartly. "Not to mention conceited."

Jeremy gave a gratified sigh and leaned back in his chair, folding his arms over his chest. "I thought I was going to have to wait forever to get a compliment out of you."

Exasperated, Maddy snapped, "That wasn't a compliment, you fathead."

"Call me whatever you like," Jeremy retorted smugly. "It's your eyes that tell the real story."

"Is that so?"

Jeremy nodded. "You'd better get used to it, sweetheart."

"I am not your sweetheart—" Maddy started, then stopped. "Get used to what?"

"The eyes never lie," he informed her. "Fact is, my dear wife, you want me so much you can hardly stand it."

"I want—" Maddy gave up. In this cocky mood, Jeremy would make sure it was a hopeless battle. "You're crazy."

Jeremy's grin didn't falter. "Crazy about you," he agreed.

"What on earth am I going to do with you?" Maddy asked, fighting hard not to match his engaging smile. "You're impossible."

"I'd be glad to offer a suggestion," Jeremy drawled wickedly.

"I'll just bet."

Suddenly his tone changed from teasing to serious. "But you're still not ready to take me up on that offer, are you?"

Maddy saw the compassion in his eyes, and she swallowed hard. She wasn't prepared for this ambush, any more than she'd been ready for the sensual onslaught he'd launched in the bathroom. She also knew, however, that Jeremy wasn't going to be put off any longer.

"I...I'm not sure *what* I'm ready for anymore," she stammered nervously, then admitted, "But I can tell you that I never expected this."

When all he did was wait patiently for her to elaborate, Maddy burst out, "Damn you, Jeremy Kincaid! You were supposed to be friendly and nice—and undemanding. That's what your brown eyes told me in that picture you sent."

"You make it sound like you were hoping for a cocker spaniel, not a man," Jeremy observed with annoyance, forgetting the fact that he'd signed up for a sweet, tractable little wife who would willingly jump to his tune. "A lapdog who would come to heel when you called, fetch you your slippers, then roll over and play dead.''

Maddy winced, knowing that his description of her expectations for a husband fell pretty close to the truth. ''Man's best friend.'' She sighed wistfully, then forced herself to bring up a subject she'd hoped to avoid for a long time to come—perhaps forever. ''Considering the past men in my life, I guess I *did* want someone safe, a man who wouldn't turn on me without provocation.''

Jeremy had never met a more provoking woman in his life, but he decided to postpone the time when they would discuss the ''without provocation'' clause as it applied to him. She was finally talking to him, intending to tell him what had gone wrong in her life, and he didn't want to say anything that might jeopardize his chances of getting the whole story. ''Is that what they did to you? Both of them?''

Resigned to her fate, Maddy started with a terse description of her relationship with Grant Parsons. ''I was fresh out of high school, and had just won a modeling contest sponsored by a department store in my hometown. First prize was a trip to New York and a free photo session with a photographer, who turned out to be Grant. He took one look at me and decided that I was his ticket to fame and fortune, but of course, he didn't tell me that, and I was too naive to figure it out. He swept me off my feet, and six weeks later we were engaged. We stayed together for almost three years, but Grant always found a reason to keep postponing the wedding.''

Jeremy watched the shadows return to her eyes and the tightness reappear around her lovely mouth, but at least he had the consolation of knowing that he wasn't the one who'd inspired them. Maddy was somewhere else, with another man, reliving something that even now, seven years later, caused her pain. "How did it end?" he asked gently, when it seemed as if she weren't going to continue.

"I'd just gotten my first cover assignment and was feeling on top of the world, when I walked into Grant's studio and found him interviewing another model. She was dark and sultry looking, and he was telling her that he needed her type to fill out his modeling stable. He told her that she was the most beautiful woman he'd ever seen—that her big dark eyes held 'the essence of feminine mystery.' "

Jeremy frowned, disappointed in her explanation. He'd expected something far more dramatic, though he could understand why a naive young woman might feel threatened by such a situation, especially one who was fresh off the farm. "So, even knowing that interviewing beautiful women was part of his job, watching him pay attention to another model made you jealous?"

Maddy shot him a scathing look. "I was jealous, all right," she admitted. "But not for the reason you think."

"Why, then?"

"Because they were both naked and Grant was conducting this so-called interview in bed."

Jeremy grimaced, ashamed of himself for assuming she would break off her engagement over something petty. "I'm sorry," he apologized. "I know that must have been tough on you, but you got off lucky. What if you hadn't found out about him until after you were married? Then you *really* would have been miserable."

Maddy gave a humorless laugh. "Grant didn't think so. He thought I should turn a blind eye to his affairs, just as he intended to do if I ever became interested in someone who could be good for my career. After all, he said, if we wanted to move in the same fast circles as 'the beautiful people,' we both had to do our part in cultivating them."

Jeremy's mouth twisted grimly. "And like any good farmer, you responded to that idea by yanking Grant Parsnip out of your life by his shallow roots."

"Parsons," Maddy corrected, though her eyes held an amused sparkle.

"Whatever." Jeremy shrugged, pleased by his ability to put that sparkle there. "He still had the brains of a turnip."

Maddy smiled in spite of herself. "I'd like to think so."

Jeremy reached across the table and placed his hand over hers. "There's no doubt in my mind."

Maddy took a deep breath, unaware that she'd taken hold of his hand, her fingers clasping his tightly, as she continued. "Two months later I met Paul Hastings. He was the account executive in charge of the Dew Drop campaign, and a much more mature man than Grant. He was urbane and sophisticated, a success in his own right, and he didn't need me to make himself look good. We worked so well together that I made the mistake of thinking that he considered me his equal."

"But he didn't."

"No, he didn't," Maddy replied curtly, then sighed. "For some reason, I always seem to attract men who either want to use me or control me, and with Grant and Paul, I never saw that until it was almost too late.''

"*Almost*, is the operative word here, Maddy,'' Jeremy pointed out. ''You struck out twice, but you didn't end up with either one of them.''

''No,'' Maddy agreed, but her expressive eyes revealed the words her mouth didn't say: *I ended up with you.*

Jeremy forced himself not to respond to her silent rebuke, telling himself that he had plenty of time to prove that by marrying him, she hadn't struck out for the third time. Maddy wasn't aware of it yet, but he'd already decided how he wanted their relationship to progress. And as soon as he knew exactly what he was up against, he intended to put his plan into action.

''So what kind of mealymouthed mush head was this Hastings-pudding guy?''

Maddy couldn't contain her giggle, but she opened her mouth in astonishment when she heard herself laugh. Not once in her two-year relationship with Paul had she ever had the audacity to laugh at him, nor had she ever met anyone else who would dare try. One of the first things Paul Hastings impressed upon a person was that he wasn't a man to be trifled with. He had the looks of an aristocrat and the old-world manners to match. By the age of thirty, he'd risen to the very top of his profession, and was still charming millions out of his clients.

Of course Jeremy had never met Paul, so he didn't know that. But even if he had, Maddy couldn't help but think that Jeremy wouldn't change his uncomplimentary description of him. Oddly enough, in comparison to Jeremy, Paul *did* seem slightly weak, not exactly a mealymouth, but a man who was rarely able to state the blunt facts. For Paul, every conversation was an opportunity to teach and inform—to pass on his exalted expertise to the uneducated.

Maddy's expression turned grim as she recalled the last thing Paul had said to her. She'd done her best to explain why she was afraid to marry him. She'd told him of her feelings concerning an equal relationship, of her fear that she was no longer herself but the person he'd created; and he'd laughed mockingly at her, as if she should have been grateful for the changes he'd brought about. Then, when she'd refused to back down from her position, he'd dismissed her from his presence like a contemptuous lord discharging a vulgar peasant.

Very well, Madelaine. If that's what you have decided, I shan't attempt to change your mind. I thought you appreciated all that I've done for you, but you have just confirmed the old adage that it is a waste of time to cast one's pearls amongst swine.

Jeremy's mouth tightened as he watched Maddy's hand slip out from under his, and his self-satisfied feeling faded abruptly as he studied her pale face. "Do you still love him?" he asked through clenched teeth.

"'Love him'?" Maddy's expression changed from bleak to fierce. "No, I don't love him. And I could kick myself for ever thinking I did."

Jeremy's brows rose at her vehemence. "You looked so miserable there, for a moment, that I just assumed you were pining away for him."

Maddy lifted her chin and stared directly into his eyes, as if she'd just resolved something in her mind—something that had been eating away at her for a very long time. "I wasn't pining for him. I was pining for a part of me that he took away, that I foolishly *allowed* him to take away."

"I gather you just got it back."

Maddy grinned at him—an adorable, impish grin that brought out her dimples to a greater degree than he'd ever seen them. Those dimples and the dazzling sparkle of her blue eyes combined into one very dangerous weapon. And Jeremy realized, with a gulp, that she was aiming her full feminine arsenal squarely at him. Suddenly *he* was the one who felt acutely vulnerable; and he didn't like the feeling one bit.

"You gave it back to me, Jeremy Kincaid," she informed him gratefully. "By forcing me to talk about this, you've made me face something I was too afraid to confront before. But now that I have, you'd better watch out!"

"Watch out for what?" Jeremy asked, his expression almost comically wary.

"Watch out that you don't underestimate my worth," Maddy exclaimed, feeling as if a huge weight had just been lifted from her shoulders. Her relationship with Grant had put a big dent in her self-esteem, but she might have recovered her confidence if Paul Hastings hadn't deliberately played on her vulnerabilities. By moving in on her so quickly after Grant, making her think she didn't know the right way to dress or talk or behave, he'd done a fine job of squashing her already shaky self-confidence. By forcing her to examine what Paul was really like, Jeremy had helped her to restore at least some of her lost faith in herself.

"Maybe I did underestimate your worth in the beginning," Jeremy admitted, thinking he was back on safe ground. "But you've proven me wrong time and time again."

Maddy increased the wattage of her smile, dazzling him until he realized that she'd switched the focus to *his* personal life.

"So, now that you've heard my tale of woe, what's the real story on you? Did you come to Alaska to mend a broken heart, or escape all the broken hearts you'd left behind?"

Actually, until very recently, Jeremy hadn't been that aware that he *had* a heart, and since he always made his lack of intentions clear to the women he'd gotten involved with, it hadn't occurred to him that he might be responsible for hurting someone. For the first time in months, he thought about Valerie Taylor, and how she must have felt when he'd announced his plans to give up his highly successful career and move out of her penthouse apartment. Although he'd never made Val any promises, they had been living together for several months, and from the way she'd reacted when he'd packed up his things, she'd been operating under the false assumption that something more permanent would eventually come of their relationship.

In retrospect, he could see how she might have jumped to that conclusion, but until he'd listened to Maddy describe her past associations with men, he hadn't realized what a complete jerk he'd been. If he told Maddy about Val or described any of the other shallow relationships he'd had in this past, she was likely to place him in the same category as her ex-fiancés.

On the other hand, he didn't want to lie to her. "To be truthful," he admitted reluctantly, "without meaning to, I've probably hurt a woman or two in my life.''

To his vast annoyance, Maddy asserted, ''That doesn't surprise me.''

Jeremy's mouth tightened. ''Meaning you won't let me get close enough to hurt *you*. Is that right?''

''Meaning that I'm afraid of being hurt again,'' Maddy corrected. ''I've learned not to trust men, and I'm having a difficult time trusting you.''

That soft-spoken admission immediately deflated his anger, and Jeremy couldn't help but respond in kind. ''I'm not a very trusting sort, either, Maddy. And I'm afraid, too. Thus far in my life, I've committed myself to my education, then to my work, and finally to owning this place. But I've never committed myself to a woman before—at least not wholeheartedly. I'm not sure I know how to go about it.''

Maddy nodded her head in understanding. ''‘Forever' is a pretty overwhelming concept, isn't it?''

''I'll say,'' he agreed, then amazed himself by keeping the conversation personal. ''I suppose when your parents died in that car crash, you were too young to know if their marriage was a happy one. But your grandparents surely hung in there. Doesn't that give you some hope that the same thing might be possible for you?''

Maddy studied his face, sensing that her answer was extremely important to him, and that his question sprang from that uncertainty he felt about long-term relationships. ''I would love it if it did, but times have changed since my grandparents' day. When they got married, there was no easy escape, and so they had no choice but to work out their problems.''

Jeremy nodded, so deep in thought that Maddy had to repeat herself before he heard her question. "Your parents didn't set a very good example for you, did they? Did they fight all the time before the divorce?"

Jeremy had forgotten just how much he'd revealed to her in his letters. At the time he'd written them, telling her things that he'd never shared with anyone else had seemed a perfectly natural thing to do, but talking face-to-face with her on the subject of his childhood made him extremely uncomfortable. About to switch the subject, he made the mistake of looking at her, and found himself saying, "My mother fought, and because he loved her so much, my father always let her win. Her problem was that she wasn't satisfied being the wife of an elementary-school teacher and she was always after him to better himself."

"How did your father feel about that?"

Jeremy didn't want to remember those days, didn't want to recall the strident tone of his mother's voice and the hurt in his father's eyes when she'd berated him, but the pictures he'd shoved to the back of his mind forced their way to the forefront. "Oh, he'd just nod, and say 'Yes, dear,' then bury his head back inside one of his history books."

"Which only added to your mother's frustration," Maddy guessed, though she had little sympathy for a woman who nagged constantly.

Jeremy laughed bitterly. "My mother loved a good argument, so one day she went out and found herself a much more worthy opponent and a far better provider than my father. We only heard from her a couple of times after she ran off with him."

"And so you set about making certain that you would be a most worthy opponent for any woman you met," Maddy reasoned perceptively. "And it also explains why you went after such a high-powered job. Your mother taught you to equate money with power."

"Maybe." Jeremy shrugged his shoulders, hating to think that he was that simple to dissect, or that the choices he'd made in his adult life had been predestined from childhood.

Maddy, however, was warming to her subject, and the way she was talking, she thought she had all the answers. "Now I know why you're still single," she declared sagely. "Taking you on would require a very strong-minded woman, and you've never found one who's been willing or able to go the full ten rounds with you."

Jeremy had had more than enough of her amateur analysis. "I'm not single," he reminded her tersely. "I'm married to a woman who doesn't even have enough guts to enter the ring."

Maddy gasped at this unexpected attack. "That was a low blow, Jeremy Kincaid!" she protested hotly.

"Well, it's the truth, isn't it?" he demanded, standing up from his chair and turning his back on her as he carried his dishes to the sink. "You want me just as much as I want you, but you don't have the courage to do anything about it."

"That's not true!"

Jeremy dumped his plates and cup, ignoring the sound of breaking crockery as he turned around, his dark eyes smoldering hotly as they settled on her startled face. "Then come here and show me," he suggested in a tone so seductive that Maddy felt the blood heating in her veins, her desire for him igniting so quickly that it stunned her.

The sudden change in his behavior knocked Maddy completely off balance. "I don't think—"

"Then don't think," Jeremy interrupted her, as he pushed himself away from the sink and came toward her. "Remember? Thinking only makes a person realize what kind of trouble they're in."

Maddy swallowed hard as she read the passionate intent in his eyes, and excitement mingled with her fear. Then, as her heart began pounding and an urgent warmth surged to life inside her, all of her earlier misgivings seemed stupid and childish. She did want him—in her bed at least—and no matter what he thought, she *was* strong enough to admit it. "Am I giving you trouble, Kincaid?" she challenged softly, as she stood up from her chair to meet him, gratified by the flicker of surprise she saw in his eyes. "What kind of trouble?"

"This kind," Jeremy growled, as he reached out for her wrist and hauled her against him. "As you very well know."

With a smile of supreme feminine satisfaction, Maddy flung her arms around his neck and matched him kiss for kiss. But Jeremy wasn't going to be satisfied with kissing this time. Then again, neither was she, so when he slid one hand to the small of her back, then lower, applying pressure there as he lifted the notch of her thighs against the fly of his jeans, Maddy arched her spine to intensify the pleasurable contact.

The provocative movement was all the encouragement Jeremy needed. With a harsh groan, he swept her up in his arms and carried her out of the kitchen. "What are you doing?" Maddy managed to ask, when instead of proceeding up the stairs to the loft, he came to an abrupt stop in the front room.

"Do you mind if we stay here by the fire?" Jeremy inquired hoarsely, not waiting for an answer as he knelt down and laid her on the soft, fur rug spread out before the hearth. "This is where I've always imagined making love to you for the first time. Will you let me?"

Even with the fire burning in the fireplace, the floor was drafty and Maddy might not have agreed with his request so quickly if her blouse hadn't already been slipped off her shoulders and Jeremy's hot gaze wasn't adoring her bared breasts. "Here or anywhere," she murmured weakly, closing her eyes as Jeremy's warm hands closed possessively over the smooth pale skin he'd exposed, lightly caressing her throbbing nipples beneath his palms.

"I've longed to see your silky hair spread out like this against the dark fur, dreamed of watching the firelight flicker over your satiny skin as I undress you," he murmured as he proceeded to do just that. "I'm on fire for you, Maddy, and I've wanted you for what seems like forever."

"I want you, too," Maddy whispered, her eyes flashing open as she heard the sound of him stripping off his own clothes. Piece by piece she watched him reveal that gorgeous body that had appeared to her in so many dreams since her arrival, and she felt as if her own skin were on fire, her body consumed in the intense heat that precedes spontaneous combustion, and within moments, all she and Jeremy could do was surrender themselves to the flames.

Seven

———

Jeremy wondered if Maddy could feel his body trembling as he pulled her into his arms, and hoped that she didn't. He'd waited so long for this moment, but now that it was actually happening, he had to show some restraint. Even before he'd lain down beside her, Maddy had reached up her arms for him, conveying her hunger; and though her eagerness delighted him, he kept telling himself to ease up. If he didn't, he was going to take her hard and fast, and he had wanted their first time together to be tormentingly slow and shatteringly intense. Jeremy was quite aware that he wasn't her first lover, but he wanted to give her so much pleasure that her previous experiences would seem like nothing in comparison. Unfortunately Maddy's soft hands were everywhere, and he could feel his loins engorged with hot anticipation.

"Hurry, please," Maddy whispered, entwining her arms about his neck. "I need you, Jeremy."

He groaned, fighting to hold on to his sanity as she arched against him, her tongue teasing his lips, her full breasts pressing into his chest. With each breath she drew, she pushed him to the very edge of his endurance, and it took every ounce of his strength to overcome the insistent urgings of his body. "I want this to be good for you, Maddy," he murmured hoarsely. "The best ever."

"It already is," she whispered back, but Jeremy didn't seem to hear. And then, as he parted her legs with his hand and he found the silken flesh between her thighs, she was beyond saying anything. She'd never before experienced such purely erotic sensations. No one had ever demonstrated this kind of concern for her pleasure, and Maddy wasn't so certain that she wanted to give a man such total control over her body. Unfortunately, Jeremy was giving her no choice in the matter.

She could feel her body respond helplessly to his slightest touch, and her basic instincts took over. The pleasure was so compelling that she couldn't deny herself, and she opened her legs wider, urging him to explore her more intimately, wanting to scream in torment when he continued to tease and tantalize, coaxing forth a molten response, then retreating just before she went over the edge.

When his mouth closed over her breast, Maddy arched her neck and parted her lips to take in more air. "No more, Jeremy...no more, please...."

Jeremy lifted his head to look at her, his features strained, but then he saw how close she was to losing control, and a searing fire flashed through him. Never before had he felt so desperate to have a woman respond to him, but soon he would be rewarded for the constraint he'd exerted over his own desire. Soon they would both reap its rewards.

"Much more," he promised her hoarsely, holding her fevered gaze with a power that was mesmerizing even as his caressing fingers bound her to him with a hypnotic rhythm of their own. "Much, much more."

Maddy could no longer contain the delicious sensations pouring through her. Her muscles clenched as she arched her body against his hand, feeling his fingers go deep inside her. She cried out, clutching Jeremy's shoulders as the first unquenchable wave of fire surged within her, and she heard him promise, "For you . . . Mrs. Kincaid . . . anything."

Not just anything, Mr. Kincaid. Everything. Maddy realized with a gasp of pleasure, then was immediately frightened by that realization. Held immobile between Jeremy's strong thighs, she felt totally possessed. She wanted the pleasure, but not to be forever bound by it. Yet that was what Jeremy was doing to her with his lovemaking. The bonds he was using were invisible, but Maddy felt them tighten around her with every touch. Jeremy seemed to know how to interpret every movement of her body, every breath she drew, and he responded to her wishes instantly.

Becoming one with him, she felt as if she were losing herself, but then Jeremy's possession and her passion intertwined to the point where she couldn't tell one from the other, and she no longer cared. Ecstasy was just beyond her reach, but not his. Jeremy knew exactly how far they had left to go, and if she trusted him enough, he would take her there.

Taking a deep breath, Maddy let herself go just as Jeremy withdrew and then plunged deeply inside her once more, setting off wave after wave of liquid heat, igniting her body with every sure stroke, ruthlessly controlling her pleasure. Then, just as the full force of her climax gripped her, he gave in to his own need, and he surged into her one final time. As Maddy gave herself up to the overwhelming sensations, she heard Jeremy cry out her name, as if he were as shattered by the brilliant explosion as she was.

Eyes closed, gasping for breath, Maddy clung to him, waiting for the last of the rippling aftershocks to grip her, fearing that the tiny currents of pleasure might never end, yet feeling disappointed when they did. She wasn't ready to release her hold on Jeremy's solid body, to open her eyes and acknowledge what had just happened between them—especially since she wasn't quite certain that her brain was ever going to function properly again. Later she might regret her uninhibited response to his lovemaking, but when she glanced down and saw Jeremy's head nestled contentedly between her breasts, she didn't want to think about anything but how good she felt.

His recovery was quicker than hers. As his breathing calmed, he shifted to one side and propped his head up on his elbow in order to look down at her face. With a tender gaze he studied the delicate pink flush of her flawless cheeks, and was overwhelmed by the magnitude of her response to him. She was still panting slightly—her incredibly soft mouth still swollen from his kisses, her blue eyes unfocused and dreamlike.

She was so beautiful. But her physical appearance was the least of what she had to offer. It was the radiant inner beauty she'd just allowed him to claim that boggled his mind. As frightened as she seemed to be of making this kind of commitment, she'd held nothing back, having given him the precious gift of herself with no reservations.

Maddy belonged to him now. And that knowledge frightened him more than he cared to admit, yet not as much as did the thought of losing her. He was committed to her, body and soul. After having made love with her, there was no way he could deny his feelings to himself—even if the time wasn't right to admit those feelings to her.

He knew what could happen to a man who risked letting a woman know how much he loved her before securing proof that his love was returned. Because his mother hadn't cared as deeply as his father, she'd always worn the pants in their family. But Jeremy was determined not to share that same sad fate as his father. He realized that Maddy was as stubborn and strong-willed as he was, but he was still the man in this marriage, and he was determined to hold his own in their relationship.

Jeremy winced as he noted a strand of silky hair curled like a golden handcuff around his wrist. Who the hell was he kidding? He didn't care who wore the pants in the family, as long as there were times like this when neither one of them did.

"That was...that was..." Maddy's voice trailed off as she gazed up at him, searching her mind for the perfect description of their lovemaking.

"Very, very nice," Jeremy supplied, but immediately regretted his inadequate choice of words when he saw the dark color flood Maddy's face.

"'Nice'?" Maddy squeaked, highly offended that he would pin such a weak adjective on the most wondrous experience of her life.

"Nice!" she repeated louder. Apparently, Jeremy had experienced much better ones, and that not only hurt her to the quick, it made her irrationally angry. "You call that nice!"

She reacted so fast that Jeremy almost didn't catch her as she attempted to scramble off the rug. Luckily, he managed to get hold of her ankle before she got away from him, and a second later, he had her outraged body pinned down underneath him. "Maybe 'nice' wasn't the right word," he conceded hastily, though he still wasn't ready to wear his heart on his sleeve for fear that she would stamp on it. "How about *terrific*?"

"I'll show you terrific!" Maddy cried indignantly, attempting to bring up her knee, but Jeremy quickly counteracted that move by trapping both her squirming legs beneath his thighs. Before he captured her wrists in one hand and pulled them over her head, she did land a few glancing blows to his shoulder, but according to the devilish grin on his face as he held her in place, no damage was done.

"Go ahead," he encouraged her, well aware that she couldn't move as his gaze lingered admiringly on her breasts. "Though I don't know what else you could possibly show me that would make me change my estimation of your considerable charms."

"Get off of me, you...you—" Maddy blustered in frustration, but before she could find the right word to call him, Jeremy covered her lips with his mouth.

He kissed her first in arrogant satisfaction, and then with a lover's persuasiveness—soothing, coaxing kisses that eased one kind of frustration, only to provoke another. "It wasn't just terrific, Maddy, it was wonderful," he whispered against her lips, then trailed a string of husky superlatives down the side of her neck, and between her breasts.

"Magnificent," he continued hoarsely, as he kissed his way toward one straining nipple and stroked the other to a throbbing point with his fingers.

He rocked his hips against her quivering thighs. "Stupendous."

He caressed the satiny skin of her breasts with his mouth. "Unique."

He entered her moist, warm body. "Unforgettable."

"Awe inspiring," he growled thickly as he moved inside her and felt her silken heat welcome him.

"Tha-that's better," Maddy managed breathlessly, as the forces of pleasure gathered strength within her and surged up between them once more. Jeremy released her arms, aware that she needed to hold on to him as her pleasure built higher and higher. Maddy shivered and shuddered in the face of the glorious storm, then surrendered herself to it with a joyful cry that was immediately matched by Jeremy's groan of utter satisfaction.

This time, neither one of them recovered very quickly. When the air around them grew chilly, Jeremy managed to grab the edges of the fur rug and wrap it about their spent bodies, but neither one of them had the energy to do more than lie there, savoring the feel of the soft warm fur against their oversensitized skin, until they heard the front door of the lodge scrape open and a man's voice declare, "The birds are returning in great number, Kincaid, and with them, the fish.''

With a startled grunt, Jeremy sat up to confront their unexpected visitor. ''Joe? I wasn't expecting you this early.''

Black eyes sparkling with curiosity, the Athabaskan Indian stepped farther into the room and declared, ''Then you still tell time like an outsider.''

Unfortunately for Jeremy, there was no place for Maddy to hide, except behind his back, which she immediately did, pulling the bearskin up and over her naked shoulders and leaving Jeremy with only one corner to cover himself.

''No fair,'' he protested, but at least he had the decency not to fight her for his proper share.

Joe, on the other hand, didn't seem to be bothered by the dictates of modesty or good manners. He sat down on the couch facing them, removed his muddy boots and pointed to Maddy with a short, stubby finger. ''Woman or wife?''

''Wife,'' Jeremy replied, and Maddy could almost feel his amused smile as she pressed herself in closer behind him so that she could peek over his shoulder at Joe without providing an embarrassing view of herself. ''Joe Senungtuk, meet Madelaine Kincaid. Maddy this is Joe, the best fishing guide in Alaska.''

Cheeks flaming, Maddy acknowledged the introduction, wishing Joe would guide himself toward another room. ''Nice to meet you, Joe.''

To her horror, Joe stood up and thrust out his hand to her, though his expression wasn't that friendly. To Jeremy, he said, ''Didn't waste much time, did you?'' Then, as another notion came to him, a tentative smile appeared on Joe's weather-beaten face. ''Perhaps I should not be so surprised. Until a man gets a few long years under his belt, he won't be satisfied with only the sweet taste of fresh fish. At least, not like I am."

Maddy stared helplessly at Joe's outstretched hand, not wanting to offend the man, but unable to return his greeting without losing her grip on the rug. Nor, after what he'd just said, was she able to convince herself that Joe wasn't well aware of the kind of activity he'd just walked in on, and Maddy knew her face was as red as a beet. As for Jeremy, he just sat there like an unfeeling lump until she gave his bare behind a pointed nudge with her knee.

"Hey!" Jeremy yelped, then got the message. "Well... Joe, we're awfully glad to see you, but before we get caught up on all the improvements we've made to the place since you left, we'd like to put some clothes on."

Joe nodded sagely. "This far north, the sun can't convince the nighttime air not to get cold even when summer comes."

When the man still didn't move, Jeremy prodded more insistently. "Maddy's an outlander, Joe. She's only been in Alaska for a short time."

For a moment it appeared as if Joe weren't going to figure out what Jeremy was trying to tell him, but then he shot Maddy an indulgent glance and stood up from the couch. Before departing for the kitchen, he chuckled, and Maddy heard him mutter to himself, "Don't see no harm in lookin'."

Jeremy heard him, too, and burst out laughing— which earned him a painful jab in the ribs. "Lighten up, Maddy," he recommended in a wounded tone. "Where Joe comes from, there's no room for modesty."

"Well, there's plenty of room for it here," Maddy retorted indignantly, and stood up. Nose in the air, she gave the rug a vicious tug and wrapped it more securely around herself, which left Jeremy seated on the floor in all his naked splendor.

"Not so you'd notice," Jeremy remarked dryly, before he located his jeans and stretched out his legs to draw them on. "Before you came, I never had to worry about my state of dress."

"Or undress," Maddy added pointedly, as she shuffled awkwardly toward the stairs to the loft.

Jeremy would have liked to follow her, and he planned to as soon as he got Joe squared away in his room. "Will you be coming back down tonight? Or should I bring your clothes to you when I come up?"

Maddy stopped with one foot on the stairs. "When you come up?"

Jeremy nodded. "Now that Joe's here, he'll be taking my room. He wouldn't mind bunking in with our guests, but they might not like it. Most of the time he smells like fish oil."

"So you'll be sleeping with me in the loft?"

Her tone sounded strange, and Jeremy searched her face, trying to decipher what she was thinking. After making love with him, she certainly didn't imagine that they would go back to the way things were before, did she? "Would you rather I didn't?"

Maddy kept him waiting for an answer for a long, tense moment, her uncertainty clear. Then, with a small, resigned sigh, she surrendered to the inevitable. "No, I guess not."

It wasn't exactly a declaration of love, but then Jeremy was prepared to accept even the slightest sign of progress. "So, will you be back down later? Joe is quite a talker, and if we let him, he'll keep us up for another hour at least."

"I'll be back," Maddy said, glad to put off the time when she would have to confront the consequences of her latest decision. Beginning tonight, she and Jeremy were going to start living like real married people, and even though she'd hoped and prayed that they would eventually sink beneath the sensual tides of connubial bliss, she felt as if she'd just been blind sided by a torpedo. After having made love with him, she didn't think she could stand it if she found out that all Jeremy needed from her was sex—especially since she'd just discovered that she was in love with him.

"You'll find us in the kitchen," Jeremy informed her, his gaze narrowed on the ashen color of her skin and the dazed look in her eyes before she turned away from him. "Maddy," he called back to her. "Are you feeling okay?"

Hearing the concern in his voice, Maddy stumbled, and had to grab the handrail to keep from falling back down the stairs. And her body wasn't the only part of her that was in danger of losing its equilibrium; her brain was teetering off balance, too. Oh, Lord! It was true! She had not only fallen in *lust* with a man who'd already proven that he was no more trustworthy than any other member of his sex; she'd fallen in *love* with him!

Considering her past two encounters with treacherous males, she couldn't afford to let her feelings for this one show. Still, when she finally dared to glance at Jeremy, the anxiety she was feeling would have been obvious to a blind man. Her face was chalk white and her eyes huge.

"Maddy!" Jeremy persisted. "What's wrong?"

"It's... It just seems like everything's happening so fast," she admitted, her expression so childlike and miserable that Jeremy wanted to scoop her up and cradle her in his arms until all her needless fears vanished.

"It's going to be okay, Maddy," he promised her gently. "Don't worry."

That assurance drew forth a watery smile. "Are... are you certain we're doing the right thing, Jeremy? Because, if you aren't, we can wait a while before we commit ourselves any further. I... I really wouldn't mind," she stammered, aware that she was talking much too fast, but unable to stop herself.

"Well, I'd mind like hell," Jeremy shot back tersely.

Maddy gulped at the angry note in his voice, and hastily offered what she hoped was an acceptable alternative. "I... I was just thinking that it might be better to look on this as the beginning of a torrid affair. Then we could still be lovers. But if the passion we feel for each other burns itself out, we wouldn't have set ourselves up for such a big fall."

Somehow Jeremy managed not to laugh. "You think it would be safer to have a torrid affair with me rather than take that giant step of actually accepting that we're married?"

Unaware of the illogic of her thinking, Maddy replied soulfully, "Much safer. Compared to love, lust is a pretty short-lived thing, and if that's all we've got between us, we need to find out before we're condemned together for a lifetime. Our partnership is working out just fine from the business angle, but we gave ourselves six months to find out if the personal side of this relationship is going to work and I think we should stick to our original plan."

Jeremy didn't remind her that business partnership aside, they'd already signed up for a lifetime sentence together and he appeared to give her ridiculous suggestion serious thought before accepting it. "Okay," he agreed. "But I'm too old to go sneaking off into dark corners in order to satiate my lust for you. I'll agree to our having a hot, passionate affair, but only if I can be your live-in lover."

Flushed by the erotic images his remarks provoked, Maddy still snatched at the offer before he changed his mind, completely unaware that Jeremy couldn't see the difference between their first arrangement and the second. "Lovers it is," she declared quickly, feeling as if a huge weight had just been lifted off her shoulders as she continued her ascent up the stairs.

A half hour later, she was back down, seated at the kitchen table and watching Joe Senungtuk finish off what was left of the venison stew. She avoided looking at Jeremy, who was fresh from the shower and wearing nothing but a faded pair of jeans. If the sight of his naked chest wasn't disturbing enough, Jeremy was well aware of her reasons for not looking at him, and that put a wicked grin on his face that didn't abate until Joe started talking.

"There's one area where spring's off to a slower start than normal, Kincaid," Joe began, pushing back his chair and patting his full stomach. "Last I heard, the body count was only a few parts less than five."

"What body count?" Maddy asked, and Jeremy stifled a groan as Joe swiftly informed her, "Those poor, dumb folks that don't make it through the winter. Their corpses come to light once the snow melts."

Just as Jeremy feared, Maddy's face went deathly pale. "How horrible!"

Joe shot Jeremy an I-told-you-so look and then elaborated on the statistics, completely ignoring Jeremy's frantic hand signals for him to knock it off. "They found a couple of hot-shot skiers that got caught up in an avalanche on Bellows Mountain, and some more remains were discovered just north of the Yukon River. Wolves ate so much of those, they can't rightly tell if they were a party of two men or three. From the sounds of it, they were out hunting and must have got trapped in a snowstorm."

Maddy was astounded by the man's insensitivity when she heard his booming laugh, but it comforted her somewhat to note Jeremy's sick expression. Unlike Joe, at least her husband still placed a high value on human life. "Those fancy guns they were toting weren't worth much to them in the end," Joe declared with relish. "But at least, the wolves got some use out of them. After the long winter we had, those beasts were so hungry that when they finished off their main course, they chewed on the wood stocks of them guns and used 'em for toothpicks."

Both fascinated and appalled by the end to Joe's grisly tale, Maddy began to question its validity. "Did that really happen?"

Jeremy jumped in before the older man could answer. "You can't believe half of what this guy tells you, Maddy. The only reason he's sharing this delightful yarn with you is to test your constitution. Before you joined us, he was telling me that there are few women outside the native tribes who can stomach the harsh life we have to lead up here and he fears you're too delicate to make it."

Joe made no attempt to dispute Jeremy's claim and subjected Maddy to a probing stare. "Now that's a fact. You don't have enough meat on your bones to interest a bear."

"What meat I have is tough as nails," Maddy retorted tartly. "Just ask Jeremy. I'm as fit for this kind of life as he is."

"Hah!" Joe scoffed.

And Maddy got the distinct impression that nothing she could say would convince him otherwise.

"You're a woman, aren't you?"

Feminist ire gleaming in her eyes, Maddy exclaimed, "Of course I'm a woman, but I don't see what difference that makes. I can do most anything a man can do."

Joe gave her a pitying look, and Jeremy wanted to strangle him as he decreed, "When the snow starts flying, being isolated does crazy things to a woman, especially one who's new to the country. It's too cold to go outside, so she gets cabin fever and starts thinking her husband ain't good enough to talk to. Even the women in my village, who were born to the Arctic, feel this need to get out and talk to other women, even if it means snowshoeing twenty miles in fifty-below-zero weather. Why, just last year, we buried a woman who got crazed in the head and couldn't wait for spring to go off visiting."

"I don't know anyone to visit," Maddy replied. "But I don't see that as such a big problem. Jeremy and I have managed to find a great deal to talk about."

This fact only seemed to add merit to Joe's contention that she wouldn't last through "the long night."

"That may be true enough now," he allowed. "But things will look different to you, come December. After a while the two of you will have said all there is to be said, and you'll start saying the same things over and over until you're so tired of hearing each other, you'll stop talking altogether. *That*'s when it really gets bad.''

"And you should know," Jeremy inserted pointedly, then informed Maddy, "he's already lost two wives that way. Months went by before he realized that they'd left him and he was talking to himself."

Joe screwed his face up into a mask of weathered wrinkles that Maddy concluded must be a smile. "Outlasted them both," he boasted proudly. "And I'll outlast the next one, too."

"Didn't you say that at your venerable old age you were completely satisfied with fish?" Jeremy asked. "Or was that just another example of how you love to exaggerate?"

Ignoring the question, Joe inquired of Maddy, "Do you really like this fella a lot?"

Since he looked as if that possibility were very hard to believe, Maddy couldn't help but laugh. "More than most men," she conceded, then added magnanimously, "In fact, I find him quite tolerable."

"Thanks a lot for that impressive vote of confidence," Jeremy groused, but as Maddy would soon come to expect from him, Joe was determined to have the last word on the subject.

"Well, I've already seen that you two do more than tolerate each other," he exclaimed gruffly. "But I'm telling you right now, you can't stay under the blankets all winter, no matter how much fun you're having. Great loving is hard to come by up here, but working out a mutual understanding is harder yet."

In the silence that followed Joe's pithy speech, Jeremy's eyes met Maddy's over the table. "I think we're beginning to understand each other very well, don't you, Maddy?''

As she saw herself reflected in Jeremy's dark, possessive gaze, Maddy wasn't sure she understood anything, but considering Joe's low opinion of the female sex, she refused to admit her confusion. "Yes, indeed, Jeremy. We understand each other very well.''

Eight

———

Jeremy was right about fishermen, Maddy thought in bemusement, as she watched their first group of guests climb into canoes. Every one of these men was a highly successful businessman, used to traveling first-class, yet as long as the grayling and trout were biting, they didn't care about the kind of bed they slept in, what meals they were served or even if there was enough hot water left for them to have a shower. In fact, as far as Maddy could tell, none of their guests had bathed since their arrival several days earlier; nor had they combed their hair or shaved.

To her amazement, they seemed to take as much enjoyment in their unkempt appearance as the size of the fish they caught, going so far as to entertain themselves at night with silly contests about the possible length of their sprouting whiskers and how long they could tolerate the fish smell on their shirts before donning new ones. Evidently poor hygiene was a necessary element of the primitive masculine ritual that must be strictly adhered to if a man was to consider himself as truly "roughing it."

Maddy didn't understand this strange notion on their part. But then, who was she to judge? Neither she nor any of her friends had ever felt the urge to see how close they could come to stabbing their big toe with a bowie knife, how much beer they could chug down in sixty seconds, or if they had the nerve to swallow a live leech. Over the past four days, however, Maddy had witnessed a group of mature and supposedly sophisticated men doing all of those crazy things, and more, in order to prove their "masculinity."

And Jeremy, it appeared, was no better than the others.

Yesterday, she'd seen him out in the middle of the lake, trying to keep his balance while balancing on the gunwale of a canoe. When he'd accomplished that feat without landing in the drink, his admiring audience had reacted as if he'd just won an Olympic gold medal. As far as Maddy was concerned, they were all crazy, and she wasn't the least bit offended that she hadn't been asked to participate in their silly, daredevil antics.

Unfortunately, Jeremy was so worried about her feeling left out of the group that he kept inviting her to go along on their fishing expeditions, unconvinced by her assurances that she would much prefer staying home. Either that, or he feared what she might decide to do with her time if he left her to her own devices for yet another day. Maddy prayed it was the former. But she had her doubts—especially when the lists of projects that she wasn't supposed to tackle without his assistance kept getting longer.

Jeremy's level of protectiveness seemed to grow in direct proportion to their intimacy; and Maddy didn't like it one bit. She'd had it with dominating men who wanted to rule her life, and if Jeremy continued in the direction he was going, their relationship was heading into some very troubled waters. It was a lucky thing for him that there'd been so many other people around them this morning, or else there would have already been a showdown.

The last words Jeremy had spoken to her before following their guests down to the lake were to tell her to stay close to the house until he got back. Apparently, he'd run across some wolf tracks on the main trail and he didn't want her taking off alone to work in the garden she'd planted. In his opinion, the small clearing that she'd toiled so hard to clear wasn't within a safe distance from the lodge, and he didn't want her taking any unnecessary chances.

Since wolf tracks were as common around Stoney Point as mosquito bites, Maddy had no intention of changing her plans for the day in order to accommodate what she considered to be a ridiculous concern. After all the effort she'd put into this project, she wasn't about to let the weeds grow up and choke out her newly sprouted plants. Therefore, the moment Jeremy's canoe disappeared around the point, she retrieved a rifle and her gardening gloves and headed down the trail to her garden.

As she knelt in the soft soil beside a row of beans and started pulling weeds, she began to calm down. Maybe she would never be able to convince most men that she was a strong and highly capable individual, but she would convince herself. And wasn't that more important? Of course, Jeremy's overprotective attitude was very frustrating, but since she didn't like to picture herself living without him, she was just going to have to be patient until he came around. Enlightenment might come slowly, but she was beginning to trust that with Jeremy, if she stood firm, it would come eventually.

This newfound patience of hers was only one of the many virtues this land had bestowed upon her. As soon as her first guests had arrived with their city-quickened talk and restless gestures, Maddy had realized how much she'd changed since the day of her wedding. Stoney Point Lodge didn't have any calendars or clocks, and without any schedule to follow, she had slowly developed a sense of inner peace.

Given all the time in the world to look, to sense, to feel, just to *be*, she'd discovered a pleasant tranquillity within herself—a serenity that had been sadly lacking during her modeling years. It was as if the glorious panorama of mountains and sky, of sweet-smelling flowers and countless creatures of the wild had cleansed her soul, allowing her to see herself clearly for the first time in a long while.

Over the past month of soul-searching, she'd dwelled less and less on her past mistakes, beginning to trust that she would never make the same ones again. She wasn't that naive girl any longer, nor would she ever leave herself open to the kind of hurt she'd experienced with Grant and Paul. Adding conviction to that resolution was her knowledge that Jeremy wasn't like either of them. No matter how autocratically he sometimes behaved, he was a man of honesty and integrity, and sooner or later he was bound to realize that she was the strong, loving woman he needed to match his own strength.

In the meantime, she would continue down the path of her own personal growth, making certain she was worthy of his love by fortifying her inner resources. Like a willow tree, she'd already learned to be more flexible, to bend with the winds and the rain instead of railing against them or breaking under the stress. As much as she needed to be considered a partner in every sense of the word, she could also see that work wasn't everything. For those who wished to be happy living here, there was no separation between work and non-work.

Besides those things necessary to guarantee survival, most everything else that could be done within a day could usually wait for the next or the one after that. The beauty that surrounded her would be there forever, and with realizing that, Maddy had stopped waiting for adventure in the wilderness in order to just sit back and *experience* wilderness. Sometimes it seemed as if by making that simple choice, she'd rediscovered the secret of the universe.

Before she'd reached this understanding, she hadn't realized that Jeremy had already done so. And now she did, which made her feel an affinity for him that went deeper than anything she'd ever felt for any man. Like her, he'd spent enough years in a synthetic environment to recognize and appreciate one that was real. He was still just as awed by the beauty around him as she was, grateful for the opportunity to enjoy on a permanent basis what was denied to so many others.

Maddy smiled as she recalled the day she'd spied Jeremy in deep conversation with Earl the ermine. In fact it hadn't surprised her at all to hear the bright, furry creature chattering back as if he could understand every word. Stoney Point was a community that contained all of God's creatures, and they lived together in a strange kind of harmony, adopting a live-and-let-live attitude toward one another that wasn't disturbed unless fear or hunger was introduced into the environment.

Hearing a rustling noise in the undergrowth surrounding the garden, Maddy looked up. "Oh, Lord, please let that be true," she whispered, as she watched a white wolf emerge from between the trees and wander into the clearing.

Upon seeing her the animal stopped midstep, staring straight at her, as if as startled by her presence as she was by his. And even when she felt her pulses race with growing alarm, Maddy had to admit that the creature she gazed at was an exquisite one. She could see that he was large for his species—an extremely powerful-looking male with a thick, luxurious white coat except along his back, where his fur had turned salt-and-pepper. His muzzle was black, as were the dark rings of fur around his eyes—slanted golden eyes; intent, glittering eyes. If not wary, then what?

Through whitened lips, Jeremy offered up a brief, silent prayer, thanking God that he'd arrived in time. Struggling to control the trembling in his hands, he lifted the rifle to his shoulder and fired a shot into the sky. Just as he expected, the wolf responded immediately to the sharp crack that split the air, and disappeared swiftly into the forest. What Jeremy didn't expect was Maddy's strange reaction to being rescued.

"Now, look what you did!" she shrieked in outrage, her eyes bright with accusation as she sprang to her feet. "You scared it away!"

"*I* scared *it*!" Jeremy exclaimed in astonishment, as he replaced the safety on his rifle and propped it up against a nearby stump. "For God's sake, Maddy! That wasn't some friendly puppy dog, that animal was the 'big, bad wolf.'"

"That may well be, but he didn't mean me any harm," Maddy protested angrily, unable to explain the silent communication that had gone on between her and the animal, but regretting its loss more than she could say. "What the heck are you doing here, anyway?" she demanded. "You haven't been out on the lake long enough to catch anything."

Taken aback by her anger, and rapidly becoming just as hot under the collar, Jeremy blustered, "No, I was only gone long enough for you to disobey my orders and jeopardize your life. All I can say is that it's a good thing I forgot our lunch basket, or right now that timber wolf would be making a meal out of you!"

"Horsefeathers!" Maddy came to a stop directly in front of him and poked one finger into his chest. "And let me remind you, Jeremy Kincaid, that I don't take orders from you or anyone else. What I choose to do or not do is my business, buster, and you don't have one thing to say about it!"

"There's where you're wrong, lady. I have plenty to say about it," Jeremy retorted, grabbing her by the shoulders and giving her a rough shake, before pulling her against his chest and hugging her so tightly that Maddy could barely breathe, let alone object.

"I'll be damned if I'll keep my mouth shut when I find you doing something this stupid," he vowed gruffly, resting his chin on the top of her head, while he slid his hands up and down her spine as if searching for invisible teeth marks. "It's my job to protect you. And that's exactly what I'm going to do."

Maddy could feel the tremors running through his body, and for the first time since he'd charged to the rescue like the fifth cavalry, she realized how afraid he must have been for her. To be fair, she had to admit that if she'd come upon him in a similar situation she would have shot first and asked questions later, but at the time, she hadn't been viewing the situation from his perspective. She'd lashed out at him for spoiling a rare and precious moment, an experience that might never come again—but Jeremy hadn't known that. He'd thought her to be in mortal danger, and understanding that, she had no choice but to forgive him.

On the other hand, she also had to make it very clear that where her life was concerned, he'd taken on far more responsibility than he was entitled to. "Jeremy, I didn't realize—" she began, in a much more conciliatory tone, but he wasn't yet ready for a rational conversation. The instant she pulled her face away from his chest in order to look up at him, his head swooped down and he captured her lips with his.

It wasn't a gentle kiss, but Maddy didn't mind. Her mood was just as tumultuous as his. When Jeremy thrust his tongue deep inside her mouth as if wanting to devour her, she flung her arms around his neck, straining toward him, affirming her own well-being by matching his ardor. She willingly allowed him to draw her completely against his powerful length, let him crush her full breasts against his hard chest. Her mouth yielded eagerly to his ruthless lips, absorbing his anger and his fear, returning his brutal possessiveness with fiery passion.

Jeremy groaned, wanting to hurt her for what she'd just put him through, yet unable to withstand the pleasure of her warm, giving mouth and the sensuous movements of her slender body rubbing against him. Her soft hands stroking his hair, her even softer lips moving hungrily under his made him so vulnerable to her that he immediately steeled himself against her loving assault by breaking off their kiss and holding her at arm's length, away from him.

"Damn you, Maddy," he swore under his breath, incensed by the hot, heavy throbbing in his loins, the intense agony of need that she was so adept at inciting within him. "Damn you for making me—"

Jeremy stopped himself from saying the treacherous *L* word just in time. Clenching his jaw to force back the confession that would render him totally defenseless, he choked out "—for making me care about you so much when you obviously don't want my kind of caring."

"Oh, Jeremy." Maddy sighed, her eyes soft with compassion as she pushed his hands off her shoulders. Slipping quickly beneath his guard, she wrapped her arms tightly around his waist. Pressing her cheek to his broad chest, she beseeched him, "Please don't think that. I *do* want your caring, but you want to wrap me up in cotton batting and keep me from doing anything that might be considered even remotely dangerous."

Jeremy stood stiffly in her embrace, denying her charge, "What you did today *was* dangerous, extremely dangerous!"

Without lifting her head, Maddy replied, "No more dangerous than some of the things I've watched you do. For instance, who was it that took off after that rabid wolverine last week without waiting for Joe, who happens to be a much better shot? And who took that header over Beaver Falls on Friday because he couldn't resist playing circus on those slippery stones? Did any of my warnings stop you?"

"But that's different," Jeremy burst out in frustration, completely forgetting how the independent woman in his arms would react to his faulty logic. "I'm a man, and I know how to take care of myself."

Maddy grit her teeth, but she didn't lessen her hold on him. "I'm a woman, and so do I," she declared tartly, then forced herself to speak in a softer tone. "Can't you see, Jeremy? That chauvinistic attitude doesn't make me feel cared for. It makes me feel as if you don't trust me, that you think I'm weak and incapable, and that you have no faith in my judgment."

Jeremy felt as if his body and brain were in violent conflict, struggling hard to decipher the opposite signals Maddy was sending out. He could feel his heart thudding painfully under the warm press of her cheek, feel her arms hugging him fiercely; and yet her words were a rejection. "No, I can't see," he ground out harshly. "Why is it so wrong of me to want to keep you safe? How else does a man show a woman he cares about her?"

"By giving her the freedom to make her own decisions and live with her own mistakes," Maddy told him, finally releasing him from her hold and stepping back to look him straight in the eye.

When she had his full attention, she shifted her gaze to the rifle lying a few feet away from them—the rifle she'd brought along to the garden. Jeremy followed her gaze, and as soon as his eyes noticed the gun, she added gently, "By treating her as his equal and trusting in her ability to take care of herself."

Jeremy stared at the rifle for several seconds, then reluctantly drew his sheepish gaze back to her. "You were armed," he informed her unnecessarily.

Maddy nodded. "I got your message this morning loud and clear. If I did happen to run into a wolf, I was going to be prepared. As it happened, that wolf wasn't interested in eating me for lunch, so I didn't need the gun. But I was wise enough to bring it along with me."

Jeremy cleared his throat. "So you were," he allowed meekly, then tried to appease her with one of his nonstop dimpled smiles. "I'm sorry, Maddy. I realize now that I wasn't giving you enough credit, but most women like it when a man plays protector, even if he *does* get a trifle heavy-handed."

"Come now, a 'trifle'?" Maddy asked, then laughed at Jeremy's dramatically wounded expression. "Okay, you idiot, you can continue in your role as the big, strong hero, but only if I get to play the feisty, strong-willed heroine."

Jeremy thought that proposition over for several seconds, a wicked sparkle coming into his dark eyes as he agreed. "I guess I can live with that," he said, then reached out and pulled her toward him. Maddy's lips parted in a startled gasp as Jeremy bent her over his arm and proceeded to kiss her in his best, movie-idol manner. "How was that, my strong-willed heroine? Do you feel like swooning?" he asked when he finally allowed her to come up for air.

Using her own dimples to her best advantage, Maddy retorted, "We feisty types never swoon in front of the hero. We kiss him back." Which she promptly did, and when she got through with him, Maddy found it immensely gratifying to see that Jeremy was the one who wasn't quite steady on his feet.

Hoping he'd learned something today, she walked over and picked up her rifle. "I think while you and our guests are out fishing, I'm going to make good on one of my boasts and bake some bread."

Jeremy frowned, but managed not to voice his objections to that plan. Maddy was putting him to the test, and he knew it. Even if she had yet to light that big, old wood-burning stove by herself, and had no idea how to regulate the heat, she was asking him to trust that she would be able to figure it out. "I can't wait to taste it," he said, praying that he wouldn't come home to find her delectable person burned to a crisp.

His eyes dark with gathering passion, Jeremy watched Maddy walk slowly across the loft to where he was lying in bed, the muted gold from the waning sun shimmering over her bare shoulders and breasts, and adding sparkling highlights to her light hair. She was usually much more modest around him, but apparently, tonight was different. Tonight, she was allowing him to look his fill at her beauty, taking her time before joining him. Her expression as she came closer was so seductive that Jeremy could barely swallow, and he felt as if he were choking when instead of climbing under the covers, she remained standing at the end of the bed. "Maddy?"

"Hmm?" she murmured softly, smiling into his eyes as she reached out and grabbed one corner of the sheet and slowly began pulling.

"Wha-what are you doing?"

"What does it look like I'm doing?" she asked in a low, sultry tone that heated his already heightened senses to a fever pitch.

As he felt the sheet slide down past his thighs, revealing his heavily aroused state, Jeremy cleared his throat. "If I didn't know better, I'd think you were trying to seduce me."

"Is it working?" Maddy asked, still smiling her siren smile as she trailed one finger along his inner calf.

"What does it look like?" Jeremy managed to answer, before she knelt down between his thighs and launched her full arsenal of sensuous weapons on his poor, supine body. Well, supine at least, he corrected himself silently, because no man on earth could endure what he was about to and feel the least bit sorry for himself.

"It's working," Maddy judged with feline satisfaction, as she sprawled wantonly across Jeremy's naked body and her hands and mouth grew increasingly bolder. Even without the physical evidence, she could sense the pleasure rising up inside him, feel it in his taut skin as she teased and tempted, soothed and caressed.

When she gently kissed the part of him that was aching most for her touch, Jeremy cried out her name, and when he couldn't take any more of the pleasure and torment, he grasped her hips and rolled her beneath him. "Now, Maddy," he groaned, as he plunged inside her, desperate to have her with him before his control shattered.

Joyously, Maddy moved to the primal rhythm, faster and faster, until that final explosive wonder enveloped them both as it always did, forcing them both to remember that whether or not it was ever acknowledged, what they were feeling was the undeniable splendor of love.

Much later, Maddy lifted her head from Jeremy's chest, a languorous smile on her face as she waited patiently for him to open his eyes. The moment his dark lashes lifted, she bestowed a quick kiss on his startled mouth. "Thank you, Jeremy," she whispered. "Thank you for allowing me to be me."

Jeremy wasn't certain, but he got the feeling that he'd made a very wise decision earlier on in the day. "You mastered the stove and did a good job on the bread, Maddy," he complimented her. "But it still makes me nervous when I think of you doing something that might get you hurt. I can't promise that I'll be this accommodating every day."

Maddy snuggled down closer to him. "Eventually, you'll get used to me doing things that the past women in your life would never even consider. What's that popular saying? 'If you're not great when you come to Alaska, Alaska makes you great or casts you aside'?"

"That sounds like you might be in for the long haul," Jeremy said, hoping that it was true, praying that she was finally going to admit that she loved him.

His prayers went unanswered. "I'll be here as long as it takes to prove that I've got the strength to make it anywhere," Maddy replied firmly, not mentioning her determination to make that stay last forever, and thus confirming in Jeremy's mind that it was only a matter of time before she left him without a backward glance.

Nine

Pete Carlisle's charter plane came in just under the
thick soup of overcast to pick up the last group of
guests for the season and fly them down to Fairbanks. In his early sixties, Pete had been flying in and
out of the bush for over forty years, transporting
hunters and fishermen, delivering groceries and supplies to isolated homesteads, hauling mail and dis-
pensing medicine to townships lacking the service of
a doctor. With a storm coming in, Jeremy had assumed that Pete would pick up his passengers and take
right off, but as usual, the man accepted Maddy's offer of tea and cookies and walked with her up to the
lodge, leaving Joe and Jeremy behind to load up his
plane.

"It was a short summer," Joe declared, as he
hoisted a duffel bag over his shoulder and waded into

the water. "I don't enjoy getting my feet wet on a day this cold."

"We never did get around to building that dock," Jeremy agreed with a shiver as he picked up two metal tackle boxes and waded in behind Joe. "That'll be first thing on my list next year."

Joe shrugged his shoulders as he stowed the duffel bag away in the hold of Pete's plane. "Guess I must be getting old. I managed without one for twenty years, but now that my rheumatism has started acting up, a dock strikes me as a real good idea."

Gazing down ruefully at his freezing toes, Jeremy laughed. "I don't suffer from rheumatism but it *still* strikes me as a good idea."

Joe nodded, following Jeremy's lead and picking up the pace as they waded back to shore for a second load. "You made a lot of changes this year, Kincaid. You and Maddy," he allowed gruffly, glancing over at Jeremy to gauge his reaction as he said, "she really took to this place, and I'll admit, she's done real good for a woman. Maybe she'll surprise us both, and decide to stay on."

Jeremy threw the last bag into the hold with unnecessary force, a desolate expression in his eyes as he faced Joe. "You were there when Matt Elliot offered her a job, and you heard the kind of salary she would get if she agreed to introduce his fall fashion line and help launch his advertising campaign. That kind of money is pretty hard to turn down."

"But she did turn it down," Joe reminded him. "Turned it down flat."

"She might not be ready to go back to modeling yet, but how many more once-in-a-lifetime offers do you think it will take before she accepts one?" Jeremy demanded, replaying the scene that had occurred after supper last night over again in his mind.

Mathew Elliot was a multimillionaire who owned several chains of West Coast department stores. Recognizing Maddy from her Dew Drop promotions, he'd been after her all week to fly out to Los Angeles and do some work for him. Mathew had accepted Maddy's refusal with good grace, and although he hadn't come right out and said it, Jeremy knew what he'd been thinking, and he tended to agree with him. "Maddy's much too beautiful, sophisticated and intelligent a woman to content herself with the rustic simplicity of a place like this for the rest of her life."

"Maybe," Joe said. "But maybe she's found what she's been looking for right here."

Jeremy wished that were true, but no matter how hard he tried, he couldn't make himself believe it. From the very first day, Maddy had been a real trooper about everything, but that didn't mean that she would be willing to make the ultimate sacrifice and agree to stay on as his wife. Actually, she'd already made that clear to him, Jeremy reminded himself as he remembered the words that had never been far from his mind since she'd spoken them: *I'll be here as long as it takes to prove that I can make it anywhere.*

If for some strange reason, she hadn't proven that to herself by now, she'd certainly proven it to him, which left Jeremy with the bitter realization that one day soon, she would come to him and try to let him down easy. It was going to be agony for him to let her go, but he would have to find the strength to do it. Unlike his father, no matter how much he loved a woman, he wasn't willing to get down on his knees and beg her to stay. He might lose Maddy, but he meant to keep his pride.

Fifteen minutes later, Pete revved up the engine of his plane, plowed over the thrashing whitecaps on the lake, and finally lifted off into the air, taking Mathew Elliot and his six business cronies back to their lives on easy street. Standing side by side on the beach, Jeremy and Maddy watched the small craft disappear into the thick grayness, listening as the humming sound of the engine was enveloped in the low-hanging clouds. Within a short time, the last note died away, leaving behind the ominous stillness that comes before the loud drama of an unleashed storm.

As he noted the wintry gray color of the clouds, Jeremy's depression deepened. He'd seen a sky like that before, and along with the other signs he'd noticed during the past several days, he realized that time was passing much more swiftly than he'd anticipated. He glanced at Maddy and, knowing that their remaining time together was fleeting by as swiftly as those fast-moving clouds overhead, his expression turned bleak. Procrastinating would only serve to delay the inevitable.

"I don't think I like the feel of this," Maddy murmured anxiously, pulling up the collar of her down-filled jacket as the wind picked up and a gust of biting-cold air blew against her face. "The temperature is dropping so fast, it's creepy."

"I saw six loons flying together this morning," Jeremy declared prophetically, staring up at the rapidly darkening sky.

Aware that there was some obscure meaning behind this ominous observation, Maddy immediately felt better. She was about to hear another hilarious tidbit of wise old Indian lore provided to them by their less-than-reliable live-in source. With an amused chuckle, she agreed to listen. "Okay, I'll bite. What does Joe have to say about this mysterious sighting of six flying loons? I'm sure it must signify something highly dramatic."

"It does," Jeremy replied in a surprisingly serious tone. "It means that it's already snowed heavily farther north and those birds are gathering prematurely to migrate south. Winter's coming early this year."

"Winter!" Maddy exclaimed in disbelief. "C'mon, Jeremy. It's only the middle of August. What ever happened to fall?"

"You know what they say about our climate. We've got two seasons. Nine months of winter and the rest of the year."

Maddy shook her head. "I don't care what they say. You can't tell me that six loons flying together is any reason to panic. Maybe those birds decided it was time for a family reunion."

"Time doesn't matter up here," Jeremy stated grimly. "Only the weather."

He sounded so morose that Maddy began to feel uneasy, and a shiver of foreboding crept up her spine as Jeremy turned away from her and started back up the path. Walking fast to keep up with his long strides, Maddy assured him, "Whatever comes, we'll be ready for it."

"Maybe. Maybe not," Jeremy muttered under his breath, but Maddy heard him.

"I don't understand what you're so worried about. You've chopped enough wood to last us a full year. I've been canning fruit and vegetables all summer, and the lodge is in much better shape than it was at the start of the season. What's the big deal if we're in for a nasty bout of bad weather?''

"Not just a bout," Jeremy repeated gruffly. "Joe woke up this morning and told me that his sense of moving game is very strong."

"Forgive me, but I don't have a clue what that means, either," Maddy declared in exasperation. "And if you're trying to tell me that we're about to be snowed in for the winter, I'm not buying it. Beneath those clouds, that sun is still plenty hot."

"The days are growing shorter all the time."

Suddenly Maddy realized that their discussion had very little to do with the weather. "What are you trying to tell me, Jeremy?"

Before mounting the front steps to the lodge, Jeremy swung around to look at her, the stark intensity of his gaze freezing her in place. "It means that our deadline has been moved up by several weeks. If we don't make up our minds about 'us' very soon, the choice is going to be taken out of our hands."

Maddy went pale as she studied his forbidding expression. Fighting panic, she inquired shakily, "Have . . . have you arrived at your decision?"

"Me!" Jeremy exclaimed harshly. "What I've decided doesn't matter. Everything depends on what *you*'ve decided."

"The heck it does," Maddy retorted, providing him with the perfect opportunity to tell her exactly where she stood in his life. "We entered into this thing together, Jeremy Kincaid, and your feelings are just as important as mine. If you want me to stay, now's the time to tell me. Or does the sight of those loons mean that our affair is over?"

Jeremy gritted his teeth, aching inside at her mention of their "affair" when all he could think about was how much he loved her. "That's the point, Maddy," he bit out. "It would have been nice to have more time together, but with the coming of winter, our affair ends. To get through the long night, we'll need a hell of a lot more than passion, and I'm not willing to invest anymore of myself in a woman who can't offer me anything else."

"I see," Maddy managed to reply, feeling as if she'd just been knifed in the stomach and was helpless to prevent her lifeblood from seeping out of her body. "So you want out."

What I want is for you to tell me that you love me, that you're ready to commit to more than an affair, Jeremy was tempted to shout. But if Maddy couldn't honestly tell him that, she was right. He *did* want out. And as soon as possible.

Hunching his shoulders against the bitterly cold wind, Jeremy gave her one more chance to say what he needed to hear. "Passion is great and caring is wonderful, but neither of those things is enough to sustain a marriage," he stated gruffly. "And no matter how much we'd like it to happen, loving somebody can't be forced."

Maddy closed her eyes to block out his expressionless features. She loved Jeremy so much, but that love still wasn't returned, and now she knew that it never would be. Through the long, pleasant days of summer, he'd been willing to accept her passion, but for him, that was all she had to offer. He cared about her, but with the onset of winter, he wanted her gone, and if that was how he truly felt, Maddy knew she couldn't stay—no matter how badly she wanted to.

"No, love can't be forced," she agreed miserably, not looking at him, and therefore missing the stark pain that contorted his features.

Jeremy jammed his shaking hands into the deep pockets of his jacket, his throat feeling raw as he emitted a hollow laugh. "Well, it sure was fun while it lasted, wasn't it, Maddy?"

"Great fun," Maddy murmured flatly, then took a deep breath. "But with winter arriving so early, playtime is definitely over."

The finality of her statement ripped him apart, and like a wounded animal, Jeremy lashed out, "I wish to God I'd taken a lesson from my parents' marriage and never placed that damned ad. Physical attraction rarely lasts very long if there's nothing else to go with it."

With a sudden flash of insight, Maddy realized what she'd been up against from the very beginning, and some of her hurt was replaced by anger. "We could have saved ourselves a lot of trouble if you'd just told me your true feelings about marriage. I've admitted that I'm afraid of commitment, but you neglected to mention that you totally reject the concept. If you had, I would never have gotten involved with you."

Grateful for the opportunity she gave him to cover his pain with rage, Jeremy challenged her. "And I should have known better than to get involved with a woman like you. We both know you've never belonged here."

Feeling as if he'd struck her physically, Maddy struggled to hang on to her pride, using it as a tourniquet to cut off the internal bleeding. "Well, your worries are all over now. I'll start making arrangements for my departure as soon as this storm blows itself out.''

Jeremy forced his reply through whitened lips, hating himself for wanting to beg her not to leave him, to give him more time when she'd just made it clear how anxious she was to go. ''There's no rush,'' he retorted snidely. ''It doesn't matter to me how long you take, as long as you're gone before winter sets in.''

Maddy wrapped her arms around herself to hold herself upright after such a shattering blow. ''We do have some legal matters that will need to be cleared up,'' she agreed, but then her control broke, and she couldn't endure any more punishment. ''But this obviously isn't the best time to get into all that. That storm's going to hit us hard any second.''

That night, for the first time since Joe's arrival, Jeremy didn't share the sleeping loft with Maddy. As for the driving, ice-cold rain that pelted the outside of the lodge for the better part of the next day, it was nothing compared to the Arctic atmosphere endured by those who remained inside. When the sun came out again, summer resumed with barely a pause. But for Jeremy and Maddy, the long, lonely days of winter had come to stay.

Maddy knew that Jeremy didn't want another emotional scene like the last one they'd endured, so she understood why he couldn't seem to find the time to sit down with her and discuss the terms for the breakup of their partnership or get down to the specifics of their impending divorce. Though the days remained seasonally warm, he avoided her with the excuse that he had only a limited amount of time to hunt for his winter supply of meat. Since he was only one man, Maddy didn't think it would take a lot to sustain him, but that didn't seem to stop him from leaving the lodge before she got up in the morning and not returning again until she'd gone to bed. After three days of this treatment, and with nothing but an undersize deer to show for his long absences, Maddy decided to confront him.

Determined not to let him escape again, she set her alarm for four in the morning, dressed warmly, and crept downstairs to await his arrival in the kitchen. As painful as this discussion was going to be, she wanted them to make a clean breast of things, believing that her wounds would heal faster if she didn't have to suffer through another month at Stoney Point, yearning for what she couldn't have. Unfortunately, as she walked into the kitchen, Jeremy was already on his way out.

"I'd like to talk to you, Jeremy," she began firmly, but he cut her off with a brisk, "Can't stop now, Maddy. There's a band of caribou over on the north end of the lake and one of them has my name on it."

Gun in hand, he strode quickly toward the front door, but Maddy was prepared for just such an eventuality. Dogging his footsteps, she swept up her parka off the peg by the door and shrugged into it as she followed behind him. "I'm going with you," she told him when Jeremy demanded to know what she thought she was doing, and to her gratification, he didn't try to stop her as she climbed ahead of him into the canoe.

Once Jeremy had pushed off from shore and begun paddling, Maddy attempted to start up their conversation again, but she had no more luck than the last time. "Shh," he whispered at her. "You'll scare them off."

Maddy shushed, but her face was a picture of what she thought about it, and Jeremy avoided looking at her as he increased the pace of his strokes. Having nothing else but the powerful motion of his arms to occupy her attention, Maddy swiveled around in the canoe in order to see if they were chasing a fictional herd or the real thing. "Oh, my!" she breathed in awe as she spotted the central figure in a band of at least fifty cows, calves, bucks and yearlings. He was a buck in his prime, tremendous in size, his coat thick and sleek. "Isn't he magnificent?"

Jeremy replied with a churlish grunt that prompted Maddy to lapse into silence again. But this time she was more than willing to sit back quietly and just look, for she'd never been this close to a wild herd. As they drifted in toward shore, Jeremy kept them downwind from the caribou, but the minute the canoe entered the shallows, the humans were sighted, smelled and sensed. In an instant, the entire band of animals turned to statues, every eye fixed on the intruders.

In return, Jeremy and Maddy focused intently on the leader of the band, the dominant one that all the others would follow. He stood at the water's edge, alert, taut and poised to move instantly. Not making any abrupt movements, Jeremy slowly lowered his paddle and reached for his shotgun. "Come to me, papa," he encouraged as he located the big buck in his sights; but when the animal responded, it caught Jeremy completely off guard.

Instead of leading his herd into the forest behind him, the leader bounded forward into the water. The others followed at once, all fifty of them.

"Yipes!" Jeremy exclaimed, swiftly lowering his rifle and shoving it under the seat ahead of him. "Pick up that other paddle, Maddy, and be quick about it. We've got to get out of here—fast."

Jeremy's harsh tone snapped Maddy out of her transfixion with the reindeer. "They're coming straight at us!"

Turning the canoe so that he was in the rear position wasted some time, but if he was going to provide any kind of protection for Maddy, Jeremy needed to situate himself between her and the swimming herd. Once that maneuver was accomplished, he tossed off his parka and put all his strength behind every stroke. But each time he looked back, the band of caribou was getting closer. He could feel the perspiration gather on his brow, but when he heard Maddy's tiny, frightened scream and saw her thrust her paddle into the water, his whole body broke out in a cold sweat.

"Oh, God, Jeremy, what are we going to do!"

"Put your whole body into it, Maddy," Jeremy ordered, making his voice firm but calm in the hope that she wouldn't panic. "We'll make faster progress if you try to match my rhythm."

Suddenly their paddles were useless for propelling them through the water and instead became the only weapons they had to keep the animals at bay. Moments later, even that effort was useless, as coming abreast of the prow, the furiously swimming herd divided itself in half, breaking formation to surround the canoe. Within seconds, they were enveloped by the caribou and helplessly swept along.

"Hold on!" Jeremy shouted, clutching his paddle as sharp-pronged antlers raked the sides of the craft and curved over the gunwale.

If she didn't want her fingers sliced off, Maddy couldn't hold on to the outside edge, so she slid off her seat and into the bottom of the canoe and wrapped her arms around the seat in front of her. She didn't dare close her eyes as the craft rocked violently from side to side, nearly tipping over one way, then the other as the milling animals bumped against its sides. The only thing keeping them from being capsized was that the canoe was caught in the very center of the swimming band, locked in by the caribous' instinctive herding together around it.

Maddy felt as if she were trapped in a moment of half adventure, half nightmare, and all she could do was stare pleadingly at Jeremy, trusting him to think of something to do that would keep them from disaster. However, with one look, she could tell that Jeremy was as shaken by this situation as she was. Like her, he was hanging on to his seat for dear life, his face without color. Then Maddy saw his frantic gaze land on a coil of rope, and he went completely berserk, standing up in the canoe and letting out a wild whoop.

Swinging the looped rope around and around over his head, Jeremy aimed for the head of the mighty buck and flung out his lasso. As if the canoe were a rodeo bronc, he spread his legs in the rocking saddle and hurled the rope into space again and again. With each try he fell short, but by pumping his legs up and down, he managed to propel the canoe closer to the leader, separating him from the rest of the herd.

He finally succeeded, and the buck immediately changed direction, dragging the canoe with him as he headed back toward shore. As the herd swerved to follow its leader, Jeremy let out more and more rope, until the canoe was in place behind the herd, riding drag. "Whoo-pee-ti-yea," Jeremy sang out in a Western twang, using the slack end of the rope as a whip to encourage the stragglers to keep up. "Git along little dogies."

Finding herself in the middle of a roundup in the Arctic required Maddy to make some rapid adjustments in her thinking about Jeremy. She'd already credited him with being one of the last Renaissance men alive, and knew he was a many-faceted, multitalented individual, but this new example of his survival skills came as something of a shock. Who would ever have thought that a boy from Brooklyn, a Wall Street stockbroker, would be such an expert cowpuncher?

The middle of a roundup was probably not the best time to ask him, she wisely decided, but she couldn't help laughing at him in astonished delight as he herded the band of swimming caribou toward the shore. Jeremy had the situation well in hand, but that didn't stop Maddy from mimicking his actions. Reaching into the bottom of the craft, she picked up a flexible fishing rod, finding pleasure in surpassing Jeremy's colorful language as she used it like a cattle prod to keep the swimming animals from upsetting the canoe. The only thing the leader of this outfit was using to keep his balance was the tension on the rope, and Maddy planned to make sure his heroics weren't rewarded by a headfirst dunk into the freezing water.

With the two of them working together, the remainder of their journey went relatively smoothly. Then, just before the big buck hit the shallows, Jeremy jerked up on the rope and released him, knowing that the others would no longer stray from their set path. Within seconds, every cow, yearling and exhausted calf had bounded onto the beach and raced after their leader into the forest.

With a wistful expression on his face, Jeremy gazed after them, then stared down at his unused rifle. "Looks like I missed my chance this time," he finally said, with a self-deprecatory expression on his face. "And he was such a damned fine buck."

"Yes, he was, but there'll be other times," Maddy assured him, her blue eyes sparkling with admiration. "If you're anywhere near as good with a gun as you are with a lasso, cowboy, I don't think you have too much to worry about."

"Some cowboy *I* am," Jeremy complained in disgust. "Surrounded by game, and I didn't get off a single shot."

"Maybe so," Maddy said. "But because of your amazing skill as a cowpuncher, those exhausted little calves didn't drown. Give them a few more years, and they'll probably grow up to be as magnificent as their father."

In the way of a true citizen of the bush, Jeremy accepted that possibility with good-natured resignation. Within the natural cycles of the wild, hunter and hunted were destined to meet time and time again. A missed chance today was tomorrow's opportunity. In Alaska, Maddy realized, every day was filled with lost chances, infinite opportunities and new lessons to learn.

"To tell you the truth, I was more worried about us than those calves," Jeremy admitted as he sat down on his seat. "For a while there, I wasn't so sure we were going to make it."

"Until you transformed yourself into Bronco Billy, I wasn't that certain, either," Maddy said, wondering how she was ever going to be able to leave such a wonderfully ingenious man. "Where did you ever learn to throw a rope like that?"

Jeremy's grin was sheepish. "Like every kid on my block, I wanted to be a rootin' tootin' cowboy when I grew up, so I saved up the box tops of my cereal until I had enough to send away for my official Roy Rogers lariat. Before I gave up on that dream, I'd lassoed every fire hydrant and stray dog in the neighborhood."

"Lucky for us that you did," Maddy declared, laughing at the picture he painted of himself. "I guess we never really know when a childhood pastime will come in handy."

Jeremy didn't look at her as he dipped his paddle into the water and began a steady stroking, but Maddy heard every word he said to the watery depths of the lake, and his ragged tone soothed the hurting places inside her like a healing balm as she heard him say, "I just thank God that you weren't hurt. I'd never have forgiven myself if anything had happened to you— never."

Would a man who didn't love her with the same kind of desperation that she felt for him react that way? Maddy asked herself as she picked up her own paddle and joined him in hastening their journey back to the south side of the lake. No, he wouldn't, she answered herself, then quickly proceeded to her next conclusion: she'd learned an important lesson about herself today.

No matter how difficult Jeremy made things for her, she wasn't going to give up on everything she wanted without a fight. To survive in the wild, one had to be strong bodied and even stronger willed, and use some ingenuity. But when a person found that straightforward action didn't work, one could always count upon the eternal laws of nature to come through. If Jeremy was right about the signs, winter was well on its way, and to get what she wanted, all she had to do was bide her time until it arrived.

Smiling wickedly, she considered all that she might do in the meantime to aid her cause. "Jeremy?"

"Mmm?"

"When we get home would you go with me to pick cranberries? They've reached their peak and since you tell me winter is so close at hand, I want to get them harvested right away."

Jeremy's hands clenched around his paddle until his knuckles turned white. "You don't have to do that, Maddy. I can get by this winter without the cranberries."

"But *I* want to," Maddy told him. "I hate to see them go to waste. Besides, as Joe always says, waste anything up here and it could be fatal."

Reluctantly Jeremy agreed to help her, resigned to the fact that she was determined to prolong his suffering. Watching her walk out of his life was going to be difficult enough, but now he was going to be forced to think about her every time he ate cranberries... or yellow squash... or stewed tomatoes. As he recalled how busy she'd been in the kitchen for the past several weeks, he swore to himself. She was leaving him with an entire pantry of poignant reminders to consume over the long, lonely months to come.

Ten

It's been quite a day,'' Maddy said, breaking the silence that was fast becoming oppressive.

One arm leaning against the fireplace mantel, Jeremy looked up from his in-depth study of the hearthstones, but he didn't respond to her statement. According to his grim expression, his thoughts weren't very pleasant, and Maddy sensed he'd been thinking about her. "For the most part, I enjoyed it," she tried again. And again, all Jeremy did was stare at her.

With a soft, frustrated sigh, she uncurled her legs from their tucked position and sat up straighter on the couch. After the wonderful time they'd spent together today, she'd been hoping that Jeremy would make the first move. But that hope was rapidly fading. The look on his face wasn't at all encouraging.

"At least, Joe wasn't in such a hurry to leave that he couldn't wait to say goodbye," she offered desperately, and could have shouted in relief when Jeremy finally managed to string a few words together.

"That must be due to your influence. Last year, I woke up one morning to find him long gone."

Maddy's lips curved upward in an affectionate smile. "I'm really going to miss that character. Did he say if he would be coming back to Stoney Point in the spring?"

"He'll be back," Jeremy replied firmly, searching his brain for something else to say that would keep her downstairs with him. "Can I interest you in a game of checkers?"

Checkers was definitely not the game that she'd had in mind, so Maddy glanced at the clock and frowned. "I don't think so. It's getting pretty late."

When that hint didn't foster the desired result, she added pointedly, "I'm ready to go to bed. How about you?"

Oh, I'm ready, Jeremy thought darkly. *More than ready.*

Watching the way her hair glowed golden in the firelight, the delectable movement of her full breasts beneath her clingy sweater as she stood up and stretched her arms over her head, he clenched his fist on the mantel, his eyes burning with frustrated desire. If he didn't act fast, she was going to disappear up into the loft and not come down again until morning. But what could he possibly say to her? *I know you don't love me, Maddy, but for old time's sake, would you mind making love with me one last time?*

Raking one hand through his hair, Jeremy stared down morosely into the fire. He could just imagine how she would respond to that question. Then again, it might be worth the risk just for the pleasure of seeing that vivid blue sparkle that came into her eyes whenever she was angry with him, and that lovely flush that came up on her cheeks. In the upcoming weeks, the memory of that heated flush might help to warm him, he decided, and he switched his gaze back to her.

She was on her way toward the stairs, and he almost started after her, but then he realized what he was doing—had been doing all day. Just like the animals busily collecting food to last them through the winter, he was storing up memories of Maddy. Along with all the cranberries he'd picked before supper, he'd gathered hundreds of lovely images, yet he knew that no matter what he did, he could never get enough to sustain him.

Even so, over the winter, he would bask in the memory of Maddy popping a ripe berry into her mouth, then pursing her lips in surprise when she discovered how hard and bitter it was. He would see her smiling mischievously over at him as she stole a few berries off the branch he was picking to fill her own bucket, hear her laughter as she spied a raccoon doing the same thing to her branch, and smell the delightful fragrance of her hair as she turned around to share the joke with him.

He would always remember her laughter, how she searched for the humor in every situation. No matter what kind of difficulty she found herself in, Maddy was able to continually surprise him with the depth of her fortitude. She wasn't built for strength, had the face of an angel, and yet Jeremy knew he couldn't hope for a better mate or partner.

This morning, in the midst of a life-threatening situation, instead of panicking as most women would have, she'd watched him playing cowboy and laughed at his desperate actions with sheer delight. For the rest of his life, he would carry a picture of her standing up beside him in that tipsy canoe, wielding a lightweight fishing rod like a bullwhip and throwing curses over the heads of that mangy herd of caribou like an old-time mule skinner. She'd never seemed more beautiful to him than she had in that crazy moment.

"Jeremy?"

Startled by the sound of her voice, Jeremy banged his elbow on the mantel. "What?" he barked irritably, unaware of the effect his sharp tone would have on her.

"Well, you don't have to bite my head off," Maddy complained indignantly. "I was only going to ask if maybe you weren't feeling well. You've been so quiet all night, I thought you might be coming down with something."

Suddenly Jeremy was just as annoyed with Maddy as he was with himself. He wasn't coming down with something, he already had it—a terminal case of Maddy fever, and the cause of his suffering was standing on the stairs looking all sweet and innocent. "Go to bed, Maddy," he growled at her. "I'm feeling just fine."

Instead of backing off while she still had the chance, Maddy remained standing on the bottom step. "If you want me to, I could heat up some of my chicken soup for you. It's supposed to work wonders for someone who's feeling a bit under the weather."

Jeremy ground his teeth together, deliberately spacing out each word. "I am not feeling under the weather, and I don't need any of your damned soup!"

"Then what *do* you need?" Maddy asked solici-
tously, one hand moving slowly up and down the
handrail, caressing the smooth polished wood as lovingly as she used to caress him.

Eyeing the unconsciously sensuous motion of her
fingers, Jeremy's control snapped and he charged the
stairs. "If you really want to know, lady, I'll be more
than happy to show you."

Maddy let out a startled squeak as Jeremy scooped
her off her feet, but her head dropped down obediently on his shoulder and her arms came up to cling
around his neck. With only one purpose in mind, Jeremy didn't question her lack of protest and he was
blind to the small, triumphant smile on her lips as he
carried her up the remaining steps. When he got finished with Madelaine Kincaid, she was going to suffer from the same tormenting malady that afflicted
him. And *then* they would see if she still found it so
easy to leave him.

Not waiting for her agreement, he tossed her down
on the bed, then sat down on the edge of the mattress
to remove his boots. He had his back to her, but the
moment she tried to move he felt it, and with one boot
still on, he jumped up and turned around, intending
to catch her before she made good her escape.

But Maddy wasn't escaping, and what she was
doing left him standing there, stunned and speechless. Knowing Maddy, he didn't expect her to lie back
submissively and allow him to take complete charge,
but nothing could have prepared him for the seductive striptease she was putting on for his benefit, and
before he could force a single word past his thick
tongue, she stood naked before him.

"Lord, Maddy, what you do to me," he breathed, unable to take his eyes off her beautiful body bathed in a circle of light from the small lamp on the bedside table. Moonlight streamed through the windows, enhancing the bewitching picture she made. It shimmered over her flawless skin, adorning the golden strands of her hair and making them glitter and gleam about her head like quicksilver.

She looked like a Greek goddess come to life and Jeremy couldn't seem to move; could only stand there, awestruck by her beauty. As she already had more times than he could count, the lovely chameleon he'd married had once again managed to catch him completely off guard. In wonder, he gazed at her for several more seconds, but then, with an effort, he forced his eyes closed, intent on reclaiming his lost composure.

It was an uphill battle all the way, for Maddy's ability to change from mule skinner to goddess, from shrew to temptress in the space of one short day boggled his mind. She possessed an amazing talent for disarming him, but tonight, it was going to be different, Jeremy promised himself. Tonight, it was going to be *his* turn to disarm *her*. Unfortunately, it appeared that Maddy was equally determined to remain one step ahead of him.

"Make love with me, Jeremy," she whispered, smiling her most beguiling smile and holding out her arms to him as his eyes flew open. "It's only been a few days, but I've missed you so much, and we have so little time left to be together."

That last reminder was all that was necessary to force Jeremy into taking offensive action. "Then let's not waste a minute of it," he murmured huskily, though he didn't rush to take her in his arms. Two could play at this game.

Stepping over the edge of the intimate circle of light, he pulled his sweater over his head, then caught her gaze with his own as he lifted his hand with tantalizing slowness to the top button of his shirt. Maddy's eyes locked with his as he began undoing the shirt, pulling each button from its hole with a provocative slowness. He heard her sharp intake of breath and smiled wickedly as he pulled the garment free of his jeans and slid it off his shoulders.

Maddy swallowed hard, her eyes following the shirt's free-fall to the floor, but Jeremy made sure that her gaze came back to where he wanted it by pulling down very slowly on the zipper of his jeans, teasing her with the sound of each separate notch as it came apart.

When he finally stood naked before her, her lips were parted, her mouth was dry and her breath was coming in soft pants. She could see how ready for her he was, and Jeremy could see what that knowledge was doing to her. Her nipples were tight and painfully erect, her long legs trembling with the need to be one with him, but still he didn't move, and Maddy couldn't trust her legs to keep her upright if she tried to eliminate the space between them.

Of course she'd seen him naked before, but not like this, not standing before her so strong, and virilely handsome. She'd married a man of physical perfection, but tonight the sight of his incredibly aroused body took her breath away. His powerful muscles gleamed in the moonlight, his bronzed skin glowing with an inner heat that she could feel without touching him.

"No other woman can do this to me, Maddy," he murmured hoarsely, his lips curved upward in a knowing smile as she struggled for breath. "Only you."

She took a faltering step forward, the caress in his voice so compelling that she had no choice. "Love me, Jeremy," she pleaded. "Right now."

Now and forever, Jeremy declared silently, praying that he would soon be able to make such a vow out loud. In the meantime, however, he would do exactly what she said, only on his terms. Before her trembling legs gave out, he bent down and lifted her up against his chest, then laid her gently on the bed.

"I will love you, Maddy," he promised, stroking the throbbing peaks of her breasts. "I am loving you."

Arms twined about his neck, Maddy kissed him, spreading her legs to accommodate him as she waited in trembling anticipation for the flaming torch of his entry. But Jeremy held himself back, his weight upon her a heart-stopping sensation in itself as he pulled her hands away from him and moved his mouth away from her lips to her breasts. His tongue found her nipples, and Maddy moaned, running her fingers through his hair, trying to capture his errant lips before they moved lower.

Hungry for him, she needed more than the tiny kisses he pressed between her breasts, the stroke of his fingers along her hip and across the smooth skin of her belly. She was ready for him, but Jeremy wanted her half out of her mind with need, and she didn't have the strength to make him stop. When he slid down even lower between her legs and kissed her there, the heat and pressure of his mouth against her most sensitive flesh set her completely ablaze. She was his to do with as he pleased, and it was his pleasure to love her in the most intimate way possible.

By the time he poised himself over her, she was gasping, her thoughts incoherent, her body writhing.

"Do you really want this to end, Maddy?" he demanded gruffly. "Can you bring yourself to leave me?"

His questions barely penetrated.

"Tell me," he ordered, his muscles rigid with the restraint of holding himself outside of the place he was desperate to be. "Tell me you can turn your back on what we have together—on this."

"I don't want to leave you," Maddy moaned against his mouth, but the words she knew he most wanted to hear remained locked in her throat.

There could be no greater torture than this, Jeremy thought as he thrust deeply inside her, then forced himself to remain still. "That's not what you said a few days ago."

"I want you," Maddy pleaded, digging her fingers into the taut skin of his buttocks, frantically urging him to start the rhythm that would put them both out of their misery. When he still refused to move, she gasped, "It was you who said that you didn't want to invest any more of yourself in a woman who only had this to offer. I never said I was ready to leave."

Jeremy closed his eyes as Maddy arched up against him, proving how much she desired him, yet making no mention of love. He yearned for the strength to overcome the constricting pain in his heart, but his physical needs were too great and he was unable to hold himself back any longer. "Stay, then, Maddy," he ground out harshly between his clenched teeth as he drove into her welcoming body. "Stay until *you* think it's time."

On the brink of release, they both cried out with the sheer joy of it. Maddy clung to him as if she never meant to let him go, and Jeremy didn't even try to stifle the groan that was torn from his throat as the memory of this primal loving was seared permanently upon his soul.

As her heartbeat slowed to a more reasonable rate, Maddy became aware of the perspiration on her skin and the chill in the air. She shivered, but she wasn't allowed to get cold. Jeremy dragged up the quilts around them both, then reached over and switched off the light. "Warm enough now?" he queried gently.

"Uh-hmm," Maddy sighed in satisfaction, though her expression became one of impatience when Jeremy muttered sleepily. "I promise...Maddy. I'll keep you warm . . . until the snow flies."

Until the snow flies or hell freezes over, whichever comes first, she stubbornly reminded herself as she snuggled down beside him. Jeremy Kincaid wouldn't recognize a woman in love if she walked up and hit him over the head with a club, she decided. But she was far too tired for that kind of physical exertion tonight. Which was really too bad, for dragging Jeremy off into some cave by the hair and making him her prisoner of love held a decided appeal. Thus were the sensual thoughts that sweet dreams were made of, and with a beatific smile on her face, Maddy drifted off to sleep.

In the morning, however, she woke up in the midst of a nightmare. It took her some moments to realize that she wasn't lost in a fierce blizzard, fighting her way through snowdrifts as tall as Barrow's Mountain, but even when she did, her body was still wracked by shivers. At first she was too groggy to understand what was causing the cold that seeped under the blankets to chill her bare skin, but once she got her eyes open, she realized that the lower half of the bed was covered by an inch of snow. As fast as it was sifting through the rafters and drifting over the quilts, the heat of their bodies was melting it.

Maddy didn't know how long it had been snowing, but obviously it had been long enough to soak through the sheets. The roof didn't leak when it rained, but Jeremy had told her that they wouldn't be able to tell if they'd developed any serious cracks over the summer until the winter winds arrived. She'd suggested that an ounce of prevention was worth a pound of cure, but Jeremy hadn't taken that advice to heart, and this was the result.

Seemingly oblivious to the damp, Jeremy slept on, a contented half smile on his face. He looked so peaceful that Maddy hated to disturb him, but they had a problem on their hands, and when she pulled back the curtain and looked outside, she saw how big a problem it was.

The wind was blowing with a vengeance, and overnight the season had changed from summer to winter. Along with the sun, the thermometer had slipped gradually downward, providing the perfect stage for an Arctic blast to drop curtain after curtain of needle-sharp snowflakes. At least five inches of it covered the ground, a mixture of wind-driven snow and ice that coated the trees and darkened the sky to a blustery gray. Incredulous, Maddy gazed through the frost-covered windowpane, having trouble assimilating the sharp contrast between yesterday and today.

"Dammit," Jeremy swore as he came up on his knees beside her, casting away the wet blankets that had finally roused him from the best night of sleep he'd had in days. "Why the hell didn't I listen to Joe and get you out of here yesterday while I still could? Now we're trapped."

"Joe predicted this snowstorm?" Maddy asked, not daring to demand an explanation of the last part of Jeremy's outburst for fear of his reply. "Do you think he got caught in it?"

"No way. Joe knew this was coming and gave himself enough time to make it downstream to the Kantukie village. He's probably enjoying a hearty breakfast with one of his cousins. We're the ones in trouble."

Still swearing, Jeremy pushed his legs off the bed and strode naked to the highboy to find his long underwear. Without stopping to put them on, he marched over to the closet and pulled out a pair of flannel-lined pants and a heavy black wool sweater. Maddy's mouth fell open as she listened to his dark mutterings. "That was using your head, Kincaid. So desperate for one last chance to make the damnable woman love you, you ignore every lesson Joe taught you. Smart, really smart."

If she needed any additional confirmation about Jeremy's feelings for her, he was giving it to her, and Maddy sat back on the bed with a joyous smile. She could listen to this kind of sweet talk for days, but when she glanced over at Jeremy, he was glaring daggers at her as if she were solely responsible for the premature change in the weather.

Plunking himself down on the small stool near the cold stove, he snarled, "Don't you have a lick of brains? Get out of that damned wet bed and get dressed. All I need right now is for you to catch pneumonia!''

Since Jeremy's expression was as dark and stormy as the weather outside, Maddy obliged him and slid off the bed, gasping in shock as her bare feet hit a section of snow-covered floor. As she removed a pair of long john's from the top drawer of the highboy, she declared brightly, ''Great job you did on that roof, Kincaid. If we want to build a snowman, we don't even have to go outside.''

Jeremy pulled on his boots and stamped down hard on the floor. ''Don't you think I know that?'' he growled as he stood up from the chair. ''This is what I get for putting off the job all summer. I should have known this might happen. Freak things like this *always* happen up here.''

Maddy wasn't about to say ''I told you so,'' and she had the distinct impression that Jeremy would never give her another opportunity. Lips tight, he waited for her to berate him for his negligence, but when she remained silent, he headed for the stairs, barking orders over his shoulder all the way down. ''Light up the kerosene stove up there, Maddy, and the one in the living room. Then bring in a load of dry wood from the shed and get the fireplace going. After that, check around all the windows, and if you find any cracks in the chinks start repairing them. There's a gale-force wind blowing through here!''

Openmouthed, Maddy stared after him, bristling at his autocratic tone until she realized what his orders truly meant. Jeremy might not realize it, but he was expecting her to pitch in and help him do things he'd never asked of her before. As that knowledge sank in, the last of her doubts concerning their future slipped away.

Even so, if Jeremy finally saw her as his equal, it wouldn't have hurt him to ask for her help *nicely*. "And what will you be doing, your majesty, while I'm doing all that?" she called down the stairs after him.

"Fixing that damned crack in the roof!" he shouted back.

Maddy heard him stomping across the living room, then down the long hall and out the door leading to the shed. As she hurried into the rest of her clothes, Maddy glanced out the window, her expression grim as she listened to the panes rattle beneath the violent force of the wind. "Not by yourself, you're not," she muttered fiercely as she rushed down the stairs.

After fetching the extra hammer and nails she kept in a kitchen drawer, she noticed the destruction around her and shook her fist at the window. "Dang you, Earl. Must you be such a sloppy houseguest?" she demanded irately. But she didn't have time now to stop and clean up after his unwelcome animal visitation. Even though she was thoroughly annoyed with the ermine, she really couldn't blame the creature for seeking a warm shelter from the storm.

Striding purposefully through the living room, Maddy shrugged into her parka and pulled open the front door. Immediately she was hit in the face by a frigid blast of wind that took her breath away. Eyes watering, she lowered her head and pulled down the hood of her parka until it covered her forehead, but she could still feel a draft down the sides of her neck, and that was the real danger of this storm—the chill factor. Wind combined with the cold could lower the temperature by thirty degrees or more within seconds, and if Jeremy didn't want frostbite, whatever he intended to accomplish outside must be done quickly.

From Maddy's point of view, four hands were much better than two, but Jeremy didn't look very glad to see her as she rounded the corner of the lodge and found him fighting his way up the wooden ladder he'd placed up against the side wall. A bucket of pitch was dangling from his elbow and it kept banging into the wall as he struggled to move up to the next higher rung without dropping the shingles clenched under his arm. "I don't want you out here, Maddy," he yelled down at her.

"And I don't want you falling off this ladder!" she yelled back.

"Dammit! I'm responsible for the cracked pitch and loose shingles on the roof and I'll fix them," he shouted to be heard above the howling wind, as she planted herself near the bottom rung and reached out with both hands to hold the shuddering wood frame steady.

Jeremy finally gave up on a losing battle. "Okay, you stubborn little hothead, but as soon as I'm up on the roof, get back inside and do what I asked you. There's no sense in both of us freezing our butts off."

"Right," Maddy agreed, but the instant he moved off the highest rung of the ladder, she started up. Luckily the wind relented enough for her to make it to the top without fear that she was about to be blown away, but it was an entirely different story once she crawled up onto the roof. It was as if each freezing gust contained a huge claw that tore at her clothing and tried to yank her off balance. Gingerly she worked her way toward the chimney where she knew Jeremy would be working, but her progress was maddeningly slow, and she feared that he would be finished with the job before she arrived to help him.

She needn't have worried. Jeremy was having just as much trouble as she was maintaining his balance as he tried to wedge the can of pitch between the chimney and his shin without losing his precarious hold on the shingles. Just as she situated herself into a workable position, the metal top of the can blew off, almost hitting her in the shoulder as it glanced off the corner of the chimney.

"What the hell are you doing up here?" Jeremy swore, the sight of her draining all the blood from his face. By taking his philosophy of "What isn't done today can be done tomorrow" to such an extreme, he'd put the woman he loved in jeopardy, and if anything happened to her because of his stupidity, he wouldn't be able to live with himself. "Get back down there before you get yourself killed!"

Maddy could see that he was angry, but the wind velocity was so great that she was barely able to make out his outraged words. Peevishly she decided that he deserved the same kind of romantic speech she'd been subjected to earlier. "I love you, too, you big dumb lummox, and if we're going to die, we're going together," she shrieked at him, then dropped down on her knees to search for the loose shingles. As soon as she found what she was searching for, she pulled the hammer out of the back pocket of her snow pants, fumbled to get the box of nails open, then attempted to grip one in the proper place with her gloved fingers.

Finally she lifted the hammer and brought it down on the nail, failing to notice that her co-worker was making no attempt to commence his portion of the work. Once she got the first shingle nailed down, she glanced over at him, but instead of spreading pitch along the bottom of the chimney, he was just sitting there, seemingly dumbfounded. "Get the lead out, Kincaid!" she ordered. "I don't want to be stuck up here all day when we've got plenty of other things to do. Besides patching up the loose chinks in our walls, and hauling firewood, Earl got into my kitchen last night, knocking over everything and making a big mess of my clean floor."

As if surfacing from a daze, Jeremy questioned weakly, "He did?"

"He did," Maddy snapped, then scowled ferociously at him. "Dammit, Jeremy! Why aren't you wearing your gloves?"

"I took them off," Jeremy mumbled. "I can work faster without them."

"You won't be able to work at all if you get sick," Maddy informed him tartly. "Now put them back on."

"Yes, ma'am," Jeremy muttered sheepishly, and pulled on his gloves. Though his fingers were stiff from the cold, his face so numb he felt it might crack, it didn't as his lips widened with an ebullient grin. If his ears weren't already tingling from the cold, he would have pulled down his hood and asked Maddy to repeat every beautiful word she'd just said to him, but knowing his wife, she was likely to kill him if he came down with something and left her to do all the work that still needed to be done.

Besides, according to Joe, they were going to be snowed in for at least another week, and Jeremy could think of far better things to do with his time than nurse a nasty cold—far, far better things.

Compelled by an urgency that had very little to do with the weather, Jeremy spread enough pitch around the edges of the chimney to keep out a tidal wave, then snatched the last shingle out of Maddy's hand and hammered it down fast. "Break a single one of your precious bones on the way down, Madelaine, and you'll be very sorry," he warned her. "Because once we're off this roof, I intend to kiss my way through your body, and I intend to be very thorough about it."

Too happy to care about the chance he was taking with his own body, Jeremy held on to the chimney with one arm and leaned down as far as he could without falling. Maddy gasped as his face swung into view in front of hers, and her lips parted in anticipation of his kiss, but her mouth was left wanting. In true Eskimo fashion, Jeremy rubbed noses with her, then gazed down into her startled eyes. "Welcome to my world, Mrs. Kincaid, and thank you for taking the darkness out of all my 'long nights.'"

Maddy lifted her chin and returned his loving caress. "*Our* world, Mr. Kincaid," she corrected him tenderly, smiling into his eyes. "Our world."

Epilogue

The long night had come to Stoney Point. During the last week of October the sun had emerged from behind the mountains shortly after noon, rode low along the southern crest for a half an hour, then set. Two days later, it didn't come up at all, merely backlighting the mountains with a pale, pink glow.

By Thanksgiving, the entire world seemed to be in cold, dark shadow, with the sun touching only the very tips of the highest surrounding peaks. The temperature was twenty below zero. The wind was blowing at thirty knots, and there was over two feet of snow on the ground.

Maddy didn't mind the dark or blustery weather. From her point of view, all that was necessary for a memorable holiday was a huge feast, pleasant conversation, and the loving companionship of family. Even though she and Jeremy were alone at Stoney

Point, together, they would be able to meet those requirements.

By "midday," it was dark as pitch outside, but inside, the kitchen was all cheery and bright, with one noticeable exception. Jeremy had set out during the brief time of light in search of their Thanksgiving "turkey," hopefully a fat Arctic ptarmigan, but after being led a merry chase by a covey of the grouselike birds, he'd lost sight of them and had returned to the lodge empty-handed. Ever since, he'd been pouting, berating himself as a lousy shot.

As Maddy sat down across from him at the kitchen table, he grumbled, "What kind of Thanksgiving is it without a turkey?"

Maddy handed him an aperitif of sherry poured over fresh-fallen snow. "Our kind," she replied contentedly, then offered up a toast. "To us, and all the new traditions we're starting today."

Unable to resist smiling back at her, Jeremy lifted his glass and clinked it against hers. "To new traditions," he agreed. "I think I like the sound of that."

"No fresh potatoes," Maddy warned him. "Or candied yams."

"And no giblet dressing," Jeremy sighed with rapidly dwindling enthusiasm.

Maddy pursed her lips and tried a different approach. "No mincemeat pie."

Jeremy brightened at that pronouncement. "I've always hated mincemeat, and pumpkin's not that much better."

"I can't stand pumpkin," Maddy disclosed happily. "Therefore, for we polar pilgrims, it's oatmeal cookies and Arctic ice cream with wild cranberry sauce."

"And rump roast of moose," Jeremy conceded philosophically. "With instant rice, sourdough biscuits and dehydrated carrots fried in caribou fat. Not to mention stewed tomatoes and summer squash drizzled with cinnamon and hot butter."

Maddy clapped her hands together. "A feast fit for a king!"

"And his beautiful queen," Jeremy complimented, leaning over to bestow a kiss on her sherry-sweetened lips.

"Happy Thanksgiving, Jeremy," Maddy murmured breathlessly, stroking the side of his neck with the backs of her fingers as she gazed lovingly into his eyes.

Jeremy took her hand and placed a kiss in the center of her palm, his voice husky with emotion as he told her, "I've got so much to be thankful for, I could spend the entire day just counting my blessings."

It was the perfect time to tell him about one more blessing he could soon count on, Maddy decided, but Jeremy hopped to his feet before she had the chance. "That reminds me," he announced as he rushed out of the kitchen. "I've made a present for you, Maddy. Close your eyes and stay put. I'll be right back."

"A present?" Maddy exclaimed in surprise, then called after him. "Aren't you forgetting what holiday this is? Christmas doesn't come for another month."

"Then consider this one of those new traditions we're starting," Jeremy suggested after a few moments, already on his way back from wherever he'd gone. Before reentering the kitchen, however, he demanded, "Are your eyes closed?"

Humoring him, Maddy obediently complied with his wishes. "I can't see a thing."

"What do you feel?" Jeremy asked, as he placed something in her lap.

As she closed her fingers around a thick ruff of soft fur, Maddy's eyes flew open. "You made this?" she cried, gazing down in wonderment at the beautiful down-filled, fur parka, it's large hood warmly lined with water-repellent mouton.

"The one you were wearing wasn't long enough," Jeremy informed her, grinning proudly at her obvious delight with his handiwork. "And this one is also a lighter weight."

"It's beautiful," Maddy whispered, tears forming in her eyes as she considered the amount of work that had gone into making this garment. "So that's what you did with those wolf pelts."

"Couldn't think of a better use for them," Jeremy said, not telling her that he was almost positive that one of the wolves he'd shot was the same one she'd encountered in her vegetable garden. Maddy had far too soft a heart, but he'd taken some satisfaction in eliminating a very real threat to her safety. "As you know, I'm not a man to brag, but you can tell that I've made some definite improvements in the usual parka design. See those pockets? They're big and deep enough to hold all the necessities of life."

Jeremy would have continued in this vein, explaining the process he'd used to dry, scrape and tan the pelts, but then he noticed that Maddy was frowning as she stood up to hold the parka against herself. "What's the matter? Is there something wrong with it?"

"I don't think it's going to be big enough," Maddy replied thoughtfully.

Surprised and indignant, Jeremy burst out, "Not big enough! Are you kidding? That size is perfect for you."

"Now, maybe," Maddy agreed, keeping her head down so Jeremy wouldn't see her smile. "But not by the end of winter. By then, I'll probably be as big as a house."

At first that announcement was met by a dead silence, but then a light dawned in Jeremy's head, and he let out a loud whoop. "A baby!" he shouted, picking her up, parka and all, and whirling her around and around. "Honest? Are we having a baby?"

Once she caught her breath, Maddy told him, "I'd say I'm about three months along."

"A baby," Jeremy murmured in awe as he lowered her gently back to her feet. "Oh, Maddy, if I'd have known you were going to make the long night *this* exciting, I'd have married you the instant I laid eyes on you."

Maddy shook her head at his bemused expression. "You did," she reminded him.

At the sound of her merry laughter, Jeremy's brows went up. But then he realized what he'd said. "So I did," he declared, patting his chest smugly. "And I must say that was an extremely wise decision on my part."

Maddy nodded, her expression serious though her blue eyes were twinkling mischievously. "Oh, yes. It's a wise man who dares to play the fool."

Instead of returning her teasing as he usually did, Jeremy hauled her back into his arms. "A very wise man," he agreed, smiling with supreme satisfaction as

Maddy lifted her chin and parted her lips in eager anticipation of his kiss.

*　*　*　*　*

Silhouette Desire ®

COMING NEXT MONTH

#517 BEGINNER'S LUCK—Dixie Browning
Meet September's *Man of the Month*, Clement Barto. Mating habits:
unexplored. Women scared him speechless—literally. But with a little
beginner's luck, Clem was about to discover something called love....

#518 THE IDEAL MAN—Naomi Horton
Corporate headhunter Dani Ross had to find the right man for a client—
but the job title was "Husband." When she met rancher Jake Montana
she knew he was ideal—for her!

#519 ADAM'S WAY—Cathie Linz
Business efficiency expert Julia Trent insisted on a purely professional
relationship with problem-solver Adam MacKenzie. But he was
determined to make her see things Adam's way.

#520 ONCE IN LOVE WITH JESSIE—Sally Goldenbaum
Who says opposites don't attract? Confirmed bachelor Matt Ridgefield
had been content with his solitary life-style before carefree, spirited Jessie
Sager had come along. The professor had a lot to learn!

#521 ONE TOUCH OF MOONDUST—Sherryl Woods
Paul Reed was the most *romantic* man Gabrielle Clayton had ever met. He
was also her new roommate—and suddenly practical Gaby was dreaming
of moonlight and magic.

#522 A LIVING LEGEND—Nancy Martin
Hot on the trail of the scoop of the century, Catty Sinclair found only
gruff recluse Seth Bernstein. What *was* this gorgeous man doing in the
middle of nowhere...?

AVAILABLE NOW:

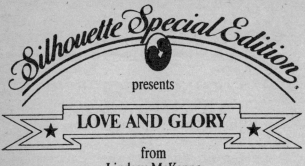

Silhouette Special Edition

presents

★ LOVE AND GLORY ★

from
Lindsay McKenna

Introducing a gripping new series celebrating our men—and women—in uniform. Meet the Trayherns, a military family as proud and colorful as the American flag, a family fighting the shadow of dishonor, a family determined to triumph—with **LOVE AND GLORY**!

June: **A QUESTION OF HONOR** (SE #529) leads the fast-paced excitement. When Coast Guard officer Noah Trayhern offers Kit Anderson a safe house, he unwittingly endangers his own guarded emotions.

July: **NO SURRENDER** (SE #535) Navy pilot Alyssa Trayhern's assignment with arrogant jet jockey Clay Cantrell threatens her career—and her heart—with a crash landing!

August: **RETURN OF A HERO** (SE #541) Strike up the band to welcome home a man whose top-secret reappearance will make headline news . . . with a delicate, daring woman by his side.

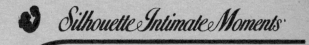
Silhouette Intimate Moments

COMING IN OCTOBER!
A FRESH LOOK FOR
Silhouette Intimate Moments!

Silhouette Intimate Moments has always brought you the perfect combination of love and excitement, and now they're about to get a new cover design that's just as exciting as the stories inside.

Over the years we've brought you stories that combined romance with something a little bit different, like adventure or suspense. We've brought you longtime favorite authors like Nora Roberts and Linda Howard. We've brought you exciting new talents like Patricia Gardner Evans and Marilyn Pappano. Now let us bring you a new cover design guaranteed to catch your eye just as our heroes and heroines catch your heart.

Look for it in October—
Only from Silhouette Intimate Moments!

IMNC-1

JOIN TOP-SELLING AUTHOR
EMILIE RICHARDS
FOR A SPECIAL ANNIVERSARY

Only in September, and only in Silhouette Romance, we are bringing you Emilie's twentieth Silhouette novel, *Island Glory* (SR #675).

Island Glory brings back Glory Kalia, who made her first—and very memorable—appearance in *Aloha Always* (SR #520). Now she's here with a story—and a hero—of her own. Thrill to warm tropical nights with Glory and Jared Farrell, a man who doesn't want to give any woman his heart but quickly learns that, with Glory, he has no choice.

Join Silhouette Romance for September and experience a taste of *Island Glory*.

NORA ROBERTS
brings you the first
Award of Excellence title
Gabriel's Angel
coming in August from
Silhouette Intimate Moments

They were on a collision course with love....

Laura Malone was alone, scared—and pregnant. She was running for the sake of her child. Gabriel Bradley had his own problems. He had neither the need nor the inclination to get involved in someone else's.

But Laura was like no other woman ... and she needed him. Soon Gabe was willing to risk all for the heaven of her arms.

The Award of Excellence is given to one specially selected title per month. Look for the second Award of Excellence title, coming out in September from Silhouette Romance—**SUTTON'S WAY** **by Diana Palmer**

Im 300-1